Magical Twilights Blueberry Beach Book 7

Blueberry Beach Novels, Volume 7

Jessie Gussman

Published by Jessie Gussman, 2021.

While every precaution has been taken in the preparation of this book, the publisher assumes no responsibility for errors or omissions, or for damages resulting from the use of the information contained herein.

MAGICAL TWILIGHTS BLUEBERRY BEACH BOOK 7

First edition. August 13, 2021.

Copyright © 2021 Jessie Gussman.

Written by Jessie Gussman.

Cover art by Julia Gussman[1]
Editing by Heather Hayden[2]
Narration by Jay Dyess[3]
Author Services by CE Author Assistant[4]

LISTEN TO THE PROFESSIONALLY produced audio version of this book – for FREE – HERE[5] on the SayWithJay Voiceworks Channel on YouTube.

Support our efforts to bring you quality audio at a price that fits into everyone's budget – FREE – check out all the FREE Dyess/Gussman audios HERE[6] **and hit the "Subscribe"** button while you're there. Thanks so much!

1. https://sweetlibertydesigns.com/services/

2. https://hhaydeneditor.com/

3. https://www.youtube.com/c/SaywithJay

4. http://www.ceauthorassistant.com/

5. https://www.youtube.com/watch?v=hn4NbpEpPBM&list=PLMynUTDTXHZraouUDUwn-hBpnXvE5ap3Uh&index=7

6. https://www.youtube.com/c/SaywithJay

Chapter 1

THE CHURCH LOOMED IN front of her like Judgment Day.

Tiffany Grant swallowed past the tight lump in her throat and gathered up every shred of courage she had.

Maybe it was an old wives' tale that when someone with a lot of sin in their life walked into a church the ceiling would fall down on them.

She was about to find out.

She'd bluffed her way through a lot of uncomfortable situations. Situations that were worse than setting foot in a church.

Much worse.

Her "friends" had always said she was cool as a cucumber.

She lifted her chin. On the outside, she was cool.

On the inside, it felt like there was a volcano erupting and people were running for their lives.

One foot in front of the other up the wide front steps. Her back to Lake Michigan, her front to her destiny.

Or death. If the ceiling thing were true.

Reaching the heavy wooden door, she almost lifted her hand to knock. Church wasn't exactly where she felt comfortable, but she'd made a decision a few months ago that she was going to turn her life around.

She'd made a lot of decisions, made a lot of changes, but the one thing she'd been putting off was her vow to go back to church and help in every way she could.

The pastor was here—at least there was one vehicle parked in the lot.

She assumed it was his.

What did she know about churches?

She hadn't been in one since she was eighteen years old.

Her old pastor was long gone, and she didn't know the one who'd taken his place.

Her true friends, the ones who loved her whether she had money or not and who lived in Blueberry Beach, had told her his name was Pastor Kane and that he was a good man. Righteous, godly, and lived a life that could be an example to every congregant who darkened his door.

The type of man who was exactly the opposite of what she was.

The blood of Christ cleanseth us from all unrighteousness.

The verse went through her head, one of a few that she'd learned since she'd turned from the life that she had been living and held her hands out for the free gift that Christ's death promised her.

It was a gift, and she'd received it, but sometimes she had trouble believing it was really true.

Faith is the evidence of things not seen.

Whatever that meant.

It was another one of those verses that she'd memorized that seemed to have significance at the time, but...that she wasn't completely sure she believed. Or she believed it, just wasn't sure she was living that belief.

How did one live something they didn't really understand?

Straightening her shoulders yet again and pushing past the lava that lapped against her ribs, she put her hand on the heavy white door and pulled.

It opened.

Whether the vehicle in the parking lot belonged to the pastor or not, the church was unlocked.

She tried to pretend she wasn't disappointed. After all, if the church was locked, she would be able to say she'd done what she said she was going to do and been unsuccessful.

Now, she had to continue on, moving forward with the plan that would change her life. Or that would show she had a changed life.

The two got murky in her head sometimes.

Wishing she hadn't sold all of her expensive clothes, had at least kept one pair of Gucci shoes, she ran a hand down her old college T-shirt and tried to pretend her loose pants didn't make her look like a bag lady.

At least they were modest.

Modesty was more important than style in her new life.

Some people said the two could coexist, but Tiffany hadn't given that much consideration when she'd been tossing clothes right and left.

She walked into the vestibule and pushed through the swinging wooden doors into the sanctuary, stifling a laugh.

The laugh was probably three-quarters because of nervousness, but the other twenty-five percent was because the swinging wooden doors reminded her of an Old West saloon.

Leiklyn, one of her friends who lived in Blueberry Beach and who owned the Indigo Inn with her, had told her that the new pastor was sincere in his calling, fervent in his messages, and had a heart to help people.

What Leiklyn had neglected to mention was the man was extremely good-looking.

He was also probably about their age.

Although she felt like she'd lived far more lifetimes than he had.

She'd seen things, and done things, that he probably didn't even know were possible for people to do.

She fought the urge to turn around and run out of the church. She had never run away from anything, and she wasn't about to start today. The changes she was hoping to make in her life were positive ones.

Running away felt like regression. Even if this was more change than she thought she could handle.

Who was she to think that she actually belonged in a church?

But the idea was short-lived, because deep brown eyes set in a darkly tanned face with a square jaw, and just enough stubble to be ruggedly appealing, looked up from the altar where he knelt.

Part of her thought it was funny that the church was set up so the pews were facing away from the lake, while the pastor would stand in the pulpit, facing the big picture window in the back and the gorgeous view of Lake Michigan.

She supposed the view could be inspiring for sermons but distracting for people listening to them. It was probably a wise decision to set the church up like that, not that it mattered. Her brain was just going crazy because she wasn't expecting the pastor to be...attractive. Or maybe more accurately, she wasn't expecting to be attracted to the pastor, but this pull, this invisible tugging that made her feet want to move forward could hardly be anything but.

She wasn't interested in attraction, physical or otherwise, nor in men in particular. She had come to Blueberry Beach to get away from men. After all, the ink was barely dry on her third divorce, and considering that she averaged less than four years per marriage, she was hardly eager to jump back into something she'd been such a failure at. It was part of turning her life around.

She didn't need a man. She didn't need marriage. But she did need to make up for the things she'd done and the person she'd been.

"Good afternoon. Welcome to Blueberry Beach," Pastor Kane said, and his voice was the kind of voice she could listen to for hours. Perfect for delivering a sermon. She'd most definitely hang on every word.

"Good afternoon. You must be Pastor Kane," she said, summoning the confidence that she'd been known for all her life.

She'd been confident in the things that she was good at. Now that she was turning her life around, she felt off-kilter, out of sorts, and definitely not confident.

"I am," he said, standing with little effort and moving toward her with the grace of an athlete.

"I'm Tiffany. I'm here to volunteer." Nothing like jumping right into it and forgoing the small talk. Not that it mattered.

She had time to make up.

His eyes blinked like her comment startled him. Isn't that what people did in church? Do-gooders? They went around helping everyone? Why in the world would he be so surprised to have someone walk in and want to help?

"Nice to meet you, Tiffany." His voice curled around her name, and a shiver traveled down her backbone.

She thought she'd outgrown reactions like that when she was about fifteen.

His hands clasped hers, and his fingers did the same thing to her hand as his voice had done to her backbone.

She managed to not snatch her hand away, but she could hardly believe this man was a pastor. She absolutely couldn't believe that Leiklyn hadn't mentioned how appealing he was.

Although, considering Leiklyn was in love with Ethan and had just gotten married a couple of months ago, she supposed it shouldn't surprise her that Leiklyn hadn't noticed.

Although... Willan could have said something.

Except Willan was in the same boat.

Maybe that was her problem, all of her friends were falling in love and getting married, and she couldn't stand it. Normally, she was the one who was getting married.

But no. That part of her life was over. She wasn't going to rush into a marriage again. Not for money, not for lust. Not for anything.

"We're always looking for volunteers. Did you have anything in mind?"

"Everything. I want to help with everything. Sign me up, put my name down, and tell me when to show up. I want to do it all."

"I see," Pastor Kane said, nodding thoughtfully. If he was still surprised, he'd managed to contain it and had a serious look on his face like this was a conversation he had every day.

As Pastor Kane studied her, she fought the urge to squirm.

"What would you say you're good at? Your strengths?" Pastor Kane asked, his voice serious and his look, while welcoming, also holding interest and consideration.

Like he was really going to listen to what she had to say.

There had not been too many times in her life when she felt like someone was actually listening to her, deeply and sincerely, as Pastor Kane was now.

But she didn't know what to say.

She didn't have any strengths. Nothing she could use at church anyway.

She could host a luncheon. Get a man to propose. Plan a pretty doggone nice wedding if she did say so herself, but none of those, except for possibly the wedding, applied to this situation.

Chapter 2

"I'M SORRY. I DIDN'T mean to stump you," Pastor Kane said, a bit of a glint in his eye.

"No. You didn't. Not really. Normally, I'm much quicker at responding, but... I just thought I would come in and help with whatever you're doing. Does it really have to be something I'm good at?"

"We like to match people up in a ministry that takes advantage of their strengths. Do you cook?"

She managed to answer without snorting. "No."

"I see." Pastor Kane nodded. "Do you sew? Or do crafts?"

She wasn't sure which was more ridiculous. The idea of her cooking or the idea of her sewing.

"No." She just discovered she had a really good acting ability, though, since she was answering these questions seriously, like there wasn't anything hilarious about them.

"Have you ever been in the hospital?"

She took a breath as though to answer, then hesitated. She wanted to lie. It was on the tip of her tongue. But this whole thing about turning over a new leaf and becoming a new person, she had to own it.

But she also realized why many people didn't want to become Christians. They had to give up their old way of life, and they knew it. Most of the time, she knew she was happier and she definitely felt better about herself living a life that was beneficial to others, but still, she really wanted to lie.

"I have. Outpatient surgery." She couldn't help it. She lifted her nose a little, putting it in the air because there was a stigma to what she was about to say. "I had a chin lift, and a tummy tuck, and also breast implants. I didn't realize I was going to have to fill out a medical form."

She added that last part because it was her old nature taking over. A little bit of sarcasm to cover what was a very sensitive subject.

"And I have some varicose veins I'd like to get taken care of, but I think I've gone under the knife enough. Shouldn't I be filling this out on a written form somewhere?" she finally asked. How long had it been since she applied for a job? She'd been a teenager at least.

The jobs that she'd done since had paid cash.

But she wasn't going back that way, and if this was what she needed to do in order to atone for her past sins, then it's what she was going to do.

Maybe she'd been too defensive to realize that her words had been slowly making Pastor Kane's jaw drop until it hung open, and he stared at her.

She got the feeling that his eyes wanted to wander, but he was keeping them firmly fixed on the spot right between her eyes on her forehead.

He cleared his throat. "I...I, um, I...I was just trying to figure out if you had been in the hospital and might enjoy visiting other people and could show compassion and empathy. I wasn't looking for the list of your...surgeries. I'm sorry I wasn't clear."

Tiffany's cheeks heated, and she could only imagine they were bright red.

She felt like an idiot.

Like she had most of the time back in school. She'd never understood what was going on like everyone else, math went over her head, reading was a chore that gave her a headache, and she could never get her dates down in history. She used low-cut, tight shirts and short shorts to take people's minds off the fact that she was stupid.

God made you the way he did for a reason.

She heard the voice in her head, and most of the time, she agreed with it, but why did everyone else get things, while she constantly misunderstood, couldn't figure out, and was the last person to know?

"Of course," she said, lifting her nose just that much higher, wishing she had her own clothes once again as a buffer between her and the world, something to make her feel better about herself, something to hide behind.

Expensive clothes gave her confidence, made her feel like she looked good, so that if her intellect was lacking, at least her physical attributes were on display, and they weren't lacking.

She'd spent a good bit of money to make sure of that.

"So... You've never been in the hospital because of illness or disease or even a car accident?" Pastor Kane asked slowly, and there was something else in his eyes now, something that had changed a little from the unguarded friendliness to a more conservative look, like he'd figured that she wasn't the typical Christian who had grown up in church and who'd never stepped a toenail off the blessed narrow way.

Good grief, she'd practically taken a bulldozer off the narrow way and run through the wilderness her entire life.

Feeling like this was a big mistake, she tried to figure out how she could turn around and leave.

Blueberry Beach was a small town, and while this wasn't the only church, it was the one that Leiklyn and Willan went to, and if she wanted to go to church with her friends, she needed to figure something out. Something that was not going to make her look like a stupid idiot again.

Ready to slink out, she stopped herself.

If she was turning over a new leaf, beginning a new life, she couldn't leave every time she felt uncomfortable or did something dumb.

She tossed her hair over her shoulder and grinned at the pastor. "I guess it's not every day that you get the lowdown on someone's plastic surgery history, is it?"

He was surprised at her change of subject, but he recovered quickly and gave a grin. "Gotta say, that's the first time. But in this job, I've kinda figured out that I should expect to be surprised, because I often am."

"That's something I might like to learn how to do. Expect to be surprised. Seems like that's the opposite of what being surprised actually means."

"Maybe I said it wrong. Maybe I should have said I brace myself and hang on, because while I know God's in control, sometimes it feels like he has me riding a roller coaster, and you know that feeling you have when you're stuck at the top of the hill, just ready to go down the other side?"

It had been years since she'd ridden a roller coaster, but she knew that feeling well, and she laughed with him. "I sure do. It's scary but exhilarating at the same time."

"That's pretty much the way being a preacher feels. Scary but exhilarating at the same time, interspersed by moments of great joy and extreme sadness."

There was something in his eyes that spoke to having seen more maybe than he wanted to, but he didn't elaborate, and she didn't want to talk about sad things. She'd been through enough hardship in her life.

None of her marriages had been about love, necessarily. Money had been the most important factor, and maybe lust. But it still didn't make it easy to walk away from something that, in the back of her head, at least, she'd hoped was going to last forever.

"I don't have any aspirations on being a pastor, but I do want to help. But I guess you've kinda figured out that...I really don't have any talent or ability."

"Do you play an instrument?"

"No." She hadn't even paid attention in music class when they'd been taught to play the recorder. She'd been too busy flirting with her seatmate.

She certainly hadn't been interested in band or orchestra, for what it was worth. Her life had mostly revolved around cheerleading, but she hadn't even been great at that.

"Do you have experience with children?"

"No."

"Cleaning?"

"No." She had a hired cleaner for most of her life, but how hard could it be? Surely scrubbing toilets was great penance. "Do you have a cleaner for the church?" She looked around. The place looked clean enough, but it only got used once or twice a week and people were probably mostly clean and in their best clothes, so it probably didn't get that dirty.

"No. People from the congregation usually clean it on a rotating schedule."

"That's great. Can you put me on the schedule?"

"Sure," he said, sounding less than enthused. "Have you belonged to a church before? Do you live in Blueberry Beach?" He asked the questions kind of tentatively, like he didn't want to offend her, especially if she'd been living in town for a while and he missed it.

"No. I just moved in," she said, giving the church another glance around. "I don't think it would be too hard to clean all this. I'm sure those other people probably don't enjoy doing it, so I don't mind taking over. What else?" she said, her natural take-control personality rising to the surface.

"Well... Actually, I think that some people probably do enjoy cleaning the church. It's seen as service to the Lord. And they feel like they're giving back to Jesus by cleaning his house."

Her head swiveled around, and she stared at him. Really? They weren't paying for their sins? They were doing it because...they loved Jesus?

That was new.

"Are you telling me I'm not allowed to clean?"

"No. I'm just saying usually people from the congregation do it, and they take turns."

"So I'm here to help. I'm always hearing about how churches want people to help. Can you give me a job?" She hadn't expected it to be this hard. But he'd been right so far—nothing she was able to do would be of any use in a church.

"I'm trying to. I'm trying to figure out what kind of job you can do."

"What were you doing right now? I'll help you." As she said that, the vestibule door squeaked, and heavy footsteps sounded behind them.

She turned around to see two teenage boys walking in.

"Hey, Pastor Kane. The bus dropped a bunch of us off. The other guys are coming in," one of the kids said.

Tiffany turned her eyes toward Kane and raised her brows. "You're doing something?"

"We're going to the children's center to visit some of the kids there. It's right behind the hospital, and one of the boys has a grandmother in the Alzheimer's wing. We're going to go see her too."

"I can help with that." That would be like penance. Visiting children, the sick and elderly.

The two boys came over and stood beside him while several more trooped in.

Pastor Kane seemed to come to a decision, and he nodded his head. "All right. You can join us."

"She's coming?" one of the kids said.

"She is, Bill," Kane said, and then he looked at Tiffany. "Tiffany, this is Bill and Cody, Ezra and Liam."

"Hi," Tiffany said, wondering why the boys were staring at her like she was doing something wrong.

"Boys, this is Miss Tiffany. She's going to come with us."

"Is she—" one of the boys started, but Kane put his hand up.

"She's going to do what we do." And his tone allowed no argument.

The boy shrugged, and Tiffany felt like maybe there was more going on than what she had realized. A sliver of that *I'm stupid* vibe from high school wrapped around her ribs. She fought it back.

Still, she'd accomplished exactly what she wanted to do, which was moving back to Blueberry Beach and immediately volunteering at the church. She had a lot of things to make up for, and she might as well get started.

Chapter 3

PASTOR KANE BURTON shook his head at himself as he walked with a group of boys into the hospital.

He'd never quite met someone so determined to help at the church in his life before. Of course, he'd only been in church ministry about five years, but still, normally getting people to help was like pulling teeth. About ten people in the church did the work of one hundred.

So when Tiffany insisted on helping, he could hardly turn her down. Even if it was a teen boy activity.

"Do you think my grandma will really be out of the hospital next week like she said?" Liam asked as they walked down the hall and across the open-air bridge that connected the hospital to the children's center just over the rise.

"I don't know. It's possible, because with God all things are possible, but I don't think that's probably what the doctor said to her."

He probably shouldn't say anything, but he didn't believe in beating around the bush with kids. He wanted to be honest and open and forthright with them so that they knew that when he said something, he was telling them the honest truth.

He found, and he himself believed, that he would prefer to talk to someone who he knew was going to tell him the truth than to someone who was just going to make him feel good.

There was nothing worse than feeling betrayed by someone who would lie to him on purpose.

He'd done enough lying in his life. It was one of the things he hated. One of the things he changed when he'd become a Christian. One of the many things.

"So we're going to see the children now?" Tiffany said, coming up beside him.

She'd hung back in the lady's room, looking uncomfortable in a hospital room with two elderly women who were in the last stages of dementia.

Both of them normally resided at the nursing home, but both of them had had falls and broken their hips. Liam's grandmother had been in for four weeks, and her hip fracture was probably only half healed, so the idea that she would be going home probably wasn't going to happen, but like he told Liam, sometimes God could do the impossible.

"We are. Have you ever visited children before?" he asked as the boys walked two abreast ahead of them.

"No. I've never visited elderly people in the hospital either, although I guess that was probably obvious."

He nodded. "You have to start somewhere, though. After you've done it a few times, you'll get the hang of it."

"She sounded like she knew what she was talking about, but...I don't think she did." She ended uncertainly, and he smiled a little at her.

"I'm sorry. I should have warned you before we walked in that she had dementia. Liam seems to be pretty much okay with it, but I try not to say too much where he can hear me," he said, his eyes on the boy in front of them, walking about twenty feet ahead and chatting with his friends.

"I get that. I was pretty upset when my grandmother died. I was in junior high. She was the one person in the world I felt cared about me."

He jerked his head over, looking at her. She snapped her mouth closed and jerked her head forward like she wished she hadn't said anything.

The lady was gorgeous. Perfect figure, but she'd confided to him where she'd gotten that, and he wondered how much of her face was perfect because of natural beauty and how much was perfect because of adjustments made by a professional.

Not that it mattered. Beauty was beauty, and he had a tendency to be leery of it. Not solely because he had been sunk deep in sin on the basis of his own looks, but also because when he'd been in that sin, he'd seen a lot of beautiful women. A lot of wicked beautiful women. A lot of beautiful women engaging in great wickedness.

Not that beauty equaled wickedness in his mind, but... Sometimes, women worked hard at making themselves look beautiful so they could be a trap for someone else.

Proverbs was clear that this wasn't something new women had all of the sudden figured out how to do, but rather something they'd been doing for thousands of years.

Men had their own sins, and he'd certainly engaged in those as well.

Still, he wasn't sure what was up with this woman who was here, seemingly from nowhere, wanting to jump in and do everything.

Ninety percent of him thought that maybe she was trying to do something to trip him up in his ministry and make him have to resign.

Ten percent of him thought that other ninety percent was terrible and couldn't figure out why he would be so distrusting of someone who seemed so sincere.

Unfortunately, he knew pastors who had fallen into temptation over women who looked less beautiful than the one who currently walked beside him.

"Death is hard. It helps when you know where you're going and can't wait to get there."

She didn't say anything, but her eyes, rather than staring straight ahead, dropped down to her feet.

They took about ten steps before she finally spoke low. "I know we're supposed to look forward to going to heaven. But I dread it."

He huffed out a breath and almost stopped short. He'd never heard anyone say they dreaded going to heaven.

"Dying?" he asked, pretty sure that's what she actually meant, even though it was not what she said.

"No. I dread going to heaven."

"Why? I mean, I know streets of gold may not be the most exciting thing to look forward to, but no more pain, no more sickness. No parting. You won't ever say goodbye to anyone again. I mean it's perfection. You'll not need plastic surgery, because you'll look perfect."

Maybe he shouldn't have said that. She had been extremely embarrassed when she realized what she'd done, that he wasn't, apparently, asking about her medical history. He still didn't understand how that misunderstanding had come about. He could hardly believe she'd never had a job interview before. Although what he was doing certainly wasn't even close to a job interview. Maybe she was just nervous.

He supposed, if she wanted to hang around the church as much as she seemed to, and he was going to be seeing a good bit of her, maybe he'd figure out her history.

Blueberry Beach wasn't a big town, and he might hear things about her, although he had the tendency to shy away from gossip.

There wasn't any more time to talk, because they'd arrived at the children's home. The boys had already knocked on the door, and Miss Kendall held it open.

"Hello! Come on in! The kids have been expecting you and are excited you're here," she said as she held the door open wider.

Kane stopped as Tiffany and he reached the door. "Miss Kendall, this is Tiffany. She volunteered to come with us today."

"So nice to meet you, Tiffany," Miss Kendall said, holding out her hand.

Tiffany shook it. "It's nice to meet you too." She peered inside. "I'm a little confused as to what a 'children's home' is."

Miss Kendall tilted her head at Kane, like she was surprised he hadn't explained, but she said, "It's new to Blueberry Beach, and we don't have many kids or staff. Actually just six children, one of whom is going back to family tomorrow."

"Is this like an orphanage?" Tiffany asked, truly perplexed.

"I'm sorry. I'm not explaining very well."

"It's my fault. I hadn't thought to tell her what exactly was going on. I can do it. It smells like you're cooking." Kane sniffed the garlic-scented air and gave Miss Kendall an easy smile.

She was a sweet woman, and he'd been told by more than one person in Blueberry Beach that they'd make a perfect couple. She would make an excellent pastor's wife, but he didn't think she was any more interested in him than he was in her. He definitely considered her a friend, though.

"Thank you. I'm pretty sure if I don't get back to my sauce, it's going to stick." Her smile never wavered as he nodded and she turned, walking back into the large building, leaving Tiffany and him standing at the door.

"I'm sorry. It didn't occur to me to explain. This children's home is a place where parents who can't take care of their kids but don't want to give them over to the government via foster care can bring them. Either permanently or just until they get back on their feet. We're completely privately funded, so we can teach them Christian values and raise them in the church."

"I see. I've never heard of anything like it."

"There aren't too many like it, really. It takes a lot of money. We're blessed to have private funding."

She was chewing it over.

"Come on in. The boys have been here plenty before, and you can watch them until you feel comfortable enough to interact."

She walked in the door, and he closed it behind them. Typically, the boys might push some trucks around, play games, or read stories to the kids.

As they walked into the big play area, he noticed Haley and Sammy over by the window, sitting with Jasmine. All three looked glum.

Checking to make sure that the boys had found something to do and didn't need his help, he said to Tiffany, "Let's go over there and you can meet some girls who would love to talk to you."

She didn't look sure, but she followed him over. Again, he wondered what her story was, since she was acting like she'd never set foot in a hospital before or done any type of volunteering.

He'd ask her later. Get her story straight from the horse's mouth so he didn't have to rely on town gossip. And he'd tell her that straight up.

Chapter 4

"HEY THERE, GIRLS," Kane said, coming over and scrunching down on his haunches, eye level with them.

After a moment's hesitation, Tiffany scrunched down as well.

"Why the long faces?" he asked.

"Jasmine has to go back to Chicago," Haley said, her long hair sitting on her shoulders, her eyes sad.

"That's good news. Her family is able to take care of her again." He tried to infuse some cheerfulness in his voice.

"We know that. We're just sad, because she's going to be leaving. And we'll miss her."

Normally, Kane had a whole repertoire of things that he could say. Things to calm, things to ease, things to make small talk when small talk was necessary.

But he wasn't sure what to say to children who knew that their friend was leaving and might never return. He could suggest they write to each other, but it's possible Jasmine's situation could deteriorate and they would lose touch.

He couldn't pull the wool over their eyes, because all three of them were savvy enough to know that. When kids came to a place like this—he'd worked at one in Chicago—they had often been abused and neglected and were wiser in the ways of the world than children should be.

"Pastor Kane, can you come here for a minute?" Liam called from about three feet away. Kane hadn't even heard him come over. He'd been trying to figure out what to say to the girls, anything that might cheer them up or take their mind off of the eminent departure.

"Right now?" he asked, not wanting to leave without at least saying something. Not saying anything was almost like admitting that they were right to be glum.

"Yeah," Liam said, sounding urgent. "Cody has his mom on the phone, and she wants to talk to you. He said she needs to talk to you right now."

Kane looked back to the girls. He hated it when his mind went blank like this, but he was wondering what in the world Cody's mom could want. She was a member of their church, though, and a single mom. He'd helped her out a time or two but never with anything urgent.

The girls were all looking at the ground, except Jasmine, who had two streaks of tears running down each side of her cheek. He wanted to reach over and brush them off and do something that would turn her look up into a smile, but nothing came to mind.

He needed to go.

"Pastor Kane?" Liam prompted.

"Go ahead and go. I've got this," Tiffany said softly.

He'd almost forgotten she was even there. She was obviously uncomfortable, and he didn't blame her, exactly, he just wasn't depending on her to help.

Her eyes were sure.

The same confidence that had entered into them when she thrust herself into the activity he had planned for the teen boys tonight.

It kind of made him smile at her confidence and her take-charge attitude.

Back at the church, he hadn't had the heart to tell her that it had been boys only.

Thankfully, none of the boys had let loose on the secret either. And while he wouldn't say that she was having a good time, at least she didn't seem to feel out of place.

He held her eyes for a moment, that same odd feeling that he'd felt back at church when he was looking at her coming over him again.

It gave him a feeling of uncomfortableness deep in the pit of his stomach. Made him feel like his past wasn't as far behind him as what he wanted it to be.

Not a good feeling when it was mostly all things he wanted to forget.

Finally, he tore his eyes away as Liam said his name again.

"You'll be okay?" he asked, unaccountably concerned for her.

"I will. Go on." Her lips tugged up just a little, and he almost got the feeling that she wanted to shoo him away.

Another odd feeling almost made him hesitate again. This was what he wanted. A helper. A woman to stand beside him in the ministry. Allowing him to do his job and supporting him.

Women like that were few and far between, and he couldn't even admit out loud that was something he craved.

He craved it because God made him to need it. To need a helper expressly fitted for him.

He shook his head. He was hardly going to find a soulmate in this doctored-up Barbie doll, with her megawatt smile, angled jaw, and baby doll blue eyes.

Funny that she would inspire that desire in him.

He jerked his head down without saying anything, straightened, and strode away.

He took the phone from Cody and spoke to Kathy.

She worked in the nursery and was scheduled to be in on Sunday. She wasn't going to be able to since she'd just been given an extra shift. The urgency was because she was using her break at work to call him and let him know.

After assuring her he would find someone to take her place, he clicked off.

In small churches, it was common knowledge that the pastor did everything. What wasn't so commonly known was that the pastor's wife usually worked just as hard.

Since he wasn't married, all of the jobs fell on his shoulders.

Sometimes, it was overwhelming.

The call hadn't taken that long, less than five minutes, but then his own cell phone rang, and when he saw it was the hospital, he answered, never knowing if it could be an emergency. It wasn't, thankfully, but was a nurse calling about a patient who didn't have any family and asked if he would visit them. He got sidetracked again, with one of the boys asking for help with a light that wasn't working, and before he knew it, twenty minutes had gone by, and he was in a completely different room before he thought to look to see how Tiffany was doing.

He had made it back down the hall and into the large children's area when he heard chanting.

Like one might hear cheerleaders doing at a football game.

His brows knit together as he put the burned-out light bulb in the trash and tried to make out the words.

He took another step and looked around the corner.

Tiffany stood in front of Jasmine, Haley, and Sammy like a cheerleading coach in front of her students, and she was leading them in what sounded like a cheer, although no cheer that Kane had ever heard.

"Give me an F!" Tiffany said in a voice just slightly lower than a shout.

The girls all screamed "F!" and threw their arms up in the air, imitating Tiffany to various degrees of effectiveness.

"Give me an A!" Tiffany called out.

The girls yelled, "A."

"Give me an M." Tiffany put one hand on her hip and raised her other arm with her hand clenched in a fist.

While the girl shouted out the M, they imitated her position.

Kane shook his head, watching. The girls were smiling, up from their drooping positions on the floor, and totally absorbed in watching and imitating Tiffany.

By the time Kane had noticed all that, Tiffany had almost gotten to the end of the cheer. "What do we have? F-A-M-I-L-Y! Family!" she said, changing her body position with each letter that she uttered while the girls giggled and struggled to keep up.

"That was fun! Let's do it again," Haley said, collapsing with another giggle on the floor, as Tiffany sat down slightly more sedately in front of them.

"Didn't you say you had a funky chicken cheer? Let's do that one!"

She laughed and started to shake her head no, but then Jasmine glanced over and saw Kane standing over by the doorway.

"Get Pastor Kane to do it!" Jasmine called, bouncing up and down a little on her matchstick legs. She would make a good chicken, Kane thought to himself, but he didn't have a lot of room to talk. His legs were pretty skinny, too.

He smiled good-naturedly as the girls all joined in calling that he should do the chicken cheer.

Universally, it seemed, everyone wanted to see the pastor make a fool out of himself, whether that was getting a pie in the face, or getting blindfolded and set on the dunking seat, or, apparently, doing a funky chicken cheer.

But he wasn't a cheerleader. He'd played sports in school, not cheered on the sidelines.

That part of his life was behind him. He was no longer using his looks or his muscles to impress anyone. But Tiffany had glanced over her shoulder, her cheeks red, her eyes sparkling, and her lips grinning. He hadn't seen such an unguarded look on her face since she'd shown up in the church two hours ago.

Her smile widened as she started shaking her head, then she got a crafty look on her face and glanced at the girls, pushing to her feet and turning to face him.

She didn't say anything to him but immediately started on the cheer.

"Come on, everybody, get your legs a-kickin'! Come on, everybody, do the funky chicken."

She kicked her legs, not high, but alternating each one in rhythm with her words.

Now she spread her feet and put her hands under her armpits, slapping her elbows and sliding one step to the side as she said, "Bok bok-bok bok bok-bok bok bok bok!"

She repeated the chicken noises, then did the cheer the whole way through again. By the time she was done, the girls were up amid giggles, although they tried to imitate her chicken stance and slide.

The rest of the kids had come over and started watching, some of them joining in, some of them just laughing, but all of them encouraging him to join her as soon as she was done.

Chapter 5

EVEN LIAM AND BILL stood, grinning at the idea.

"Come on, pastor. You always tell us not to be afraid to jump in wherever you can," Liam said, his arms crossed over his chest, almost as though he were challenging Kane as to whether or not he was actually going to do it.

Kane grinned. "What I actually always say is 'don't be afraid to jump in and help," he said, emphasizing the word "help."

"Same deal," Ezra said, taking Ryan who was riding on his back, his bare little legs sticking out, one shoe on, one shoe lost somewhere, over and standing beside Tiffany. "We're in, at least. We're not scared."

The other boys lined up, along with the children, and Tiffany didn't hesitate but started her cheer again. They locked elbows this time, although Tiffany and Cody were the only ones who were able to get their feet kicking in time with the chant.

Kane had done a lot of things to look foolish in his time as a pastor, far more than he had done before he became a man of God, but this was up there in the top five or so of things that were going to make him look especially stupid.

Nonetheless, by the time they got to the bok-boks, he had his hands tucked up, and he did the boks and slide with them to the delight of the children. He supposed the giggles and grins were worth it, and he had to admit this had been a very effective way to get the girls' minds off the fact that Jasmine was leaving tomorrow.

Tiffany had said she wasn't good at anything, and truthfully, if she had told him that she'd been a cheerleader, he probably would have fought the urge to roll his eyes, wondering what in the world a person would ever need a talent like that for when volunteering for the church.

It would have just shown how wrong he was and proven, once again, that God could use anyone and anything.

Even a funky chicken cheer.

When the cheer was over, the girls collapsed in a heap, giggling, while Tiffany grinned and unhooked her elbow from Liam and Ezra. The kids talked a bit more, and they did the cheer one more time.

The kids were begging to play a game of hide-and-seek when Miss Kendall came out and said, "All right, kids. Time to go wash up for supper. Haley, your job is to set the table today, and, Ryan, you need to move the bench over." Her face was wreathed in smiles, and her eyes looked lovingly at the children.

Miss Kendall was maybe ten years younger than Kane, but maybe the different people who had suggested that they might make a good match had been right.

She was sweet and kind and had a servant's heart. She'd given up a life of wealth and privilege to come here and open the children's home, and she was doing an excellent job. She would be a perfect pastor's wife.

They'd strolled along the lake several times together, but she didn't seem any more thrilled about him than he did about her.

Still, she was his friend, and he went over, holding his hand out. "It was good to see you. Thanks for letting us come and get the kids all wound up."

Her easy smile broke across her face as she clasped his hand. "It's always nice to see you and your boys. The kids have a great time when you're here, and they talk about your visit for days."

She had just a slight southern accent left from her time growing up in Savannah, and it added to her charm. Gracious as always, Miss Kendall turned to Tiffany and held out her hand to her. "It was good to meet you. I hope you can come back."

"I hope so too." Tiffany seemed to think better of saying anything else and snapped her mouth closed, taking Miss Kendall's hand with much more reserve and just a small tilt of her lips.

Kane hadn't met too many people who could withstand Miss Kendall's charm, but Tiffany seemed to view her as competition or an antagonist. Definitely there was mistrust in her eyes.

Interestingly, that made Kane curious. Why would she look suspiciously at someone as sweet and nice as Miss Kendall?

"You are certainly welcome anytime. And if you're looking for something to do, we're always looking for help."

"I'll keep that in mind," Tiffany said, making it sound like she wouldn't give it another thought.

The conversation felt stilted, so Kane stepped in. "This home just opened earlier this fall. There's a larger one in South Chicago, but the kids there only have the city experience, and an anonymous donor here in Blueberry Beach gave a large sum of money to fix this place." He used a hand and swept it around, indicating the building they were in. "It was an old warehouse that wasn't bulldozed when the hospital went in, and it's only partially fixed up now, but there's plans to expand next spring and the possibility of having more children come."

"We can always use more help," Miss Kendall added with a small laugh that sounded sweet and musical.

"I see," Tiffany said, still sounding and looking completely disinterested.

"Okay, boys, let's head out," Kane said finally, unsure what was going on with Tiffany but figuring it might be something he needed to get to the bottom of.

She'd been fine with him, mostly, other than her awkward degeneration into her history of plastic surgery, good with the boys, and excellent with the kids. He supposed he'd seen once or twice women who didn't seem to be able to get along with other women, but they weren't typically women that were in church.

He'd seen them more in his previous profession, the one he tried not to think about, other than knowing he didn't want to go back to it and appreciating what he'd been saved from.

They walked out, the boys gathering around them and saying, "We're playing ping-pong now?"

Ezra said, "Pizza first, right?"

"And soda," Cody said. "My mom doesn't let me have soda except when I'm doing something with the church."

"That's because she doesn't know you're having soda."

"And she's not finding out," Bill said, giving Ezra a dark look.

"I didn't know your mom doesn't let you drink soda," Kane said easily as they walked to the church van.

"That's because he wasn't going to tell you, and he made us all promise not to tell you either," Liam said with a smirk at Cody.

"I'll tell her today when I go home. But I know it's okay. As long as I'm at church, she's okay. After all, I could be out drinking beer with my friends instead of soda with the pastor."

"That's a good line. My parents never gave a flip what I did, but I can imagine that line would convince a parent to let their kid have a can of soda every once in a while," Tiffany said, her look serious but her eyes smiling at Cody.

Interesting that her parents never gave a flip. He tucked that info away.

"You must have been a cheerleader," Kane said as they reached the van. He debated with himself for just a moment before he continued around and opened her door. It was typically considered a romantic gesture, he knew, but also a chivalrous one, and while it wasn't one that he had been brought up to do, he felt that when a person had a choice of whether or not to be kind, it was never wrong to choose kindness.

Her brow shot way up when she realized what he was doing, but she mumbled a thank you as she got in and didn't yell at him or berate him, telling him that she could open it herself, that she wasn't completely helpless.

Maybe because it surprised her, or maybe because she was trying to change what she used to be too.

He had the feeling, had gotten it from the beginning almost, that she wasn't a churched person but had found Christ and was trying to change.

He couldn't fault her. Plenty of Christians spent their entire lives trying to figure out how to live like a Christian.

It wasn't easy for someone to start midlife and completely change their life, giving up the old things that they loved and that pulled them and finding new things to love and new things to build a new life on.

With God's help, all things were possible, but it still wasn't easy. Otherwise, everyone would do it.

He started to close the door, his eyes going toward the western sky, where the sun had set, and darkness was starting to settle down, that magical time between daylight and dark, the sparkling twilight that shimmered and whispered and wrapped around him.

His favorite time of day, where two became one. The dark of the night and the light of the day shared space for just a bit before day slipped away and night emerged victorious.

It always put him in a contemplative mood, but there was no time for that tonight, so he shook it off.

Tiffany snapped her seat belt and looked up, surprise in her eyes, like she was wondering why he hadn't shut the door and moved on as the boys climbed in the back.

"You're welcome to stay at the church and play ping-pong with us if you want to. I did order pizza, and it should be ready for me to pick up on our way home."

She kind of seemed like the type of woman who might be on a no-carb diet, so he wasn't too surprised when she shook her head.

"I can't. As tempting as that sounds. I...I'll be working the desk in the evening at the Indigo Inn, through midnight. I need to go."

Maybe their eyes would have met and held, maybe the shimmering waves of orange sunlight, the whisper of the wind, the trail of darkness as it draped around them would have created a spell, a magical cocoon for the two of them to get lost in, but Liam called from the back seat, "She's just afraid we'll beat her butt."

"I've never played ping-pong before, so I'm probably terrible at it. I'm not exactly known for my coordination." Tiffany didn't seem to care if they would beat her or not.

"You were pretty coordinated during your cheerleading session," Kane pointed out.

"I was imitating a chicken. That doesn't take coordination, that just takes brass. I have that. Haven't you figured that out?" She lifted an eyebrow, and it was a challenge.

He nodded slowly. "I did." He met her raised brow with a challenging look of his own. "I liked it."

Chapter 6

WHEN TIFFANY WALKED into the Indigo Inn, she wasn't surprised to see that there was no one at the desk.

Willan and Leiklyn had told her that the evening shift was a hard one for them to cover because of their families.

She had just set her purse down behind it when Leiklyn came bustling out, her son, Trent, following at her heels.

"Tiffany! You made it," she said, throwing her arms out and grabbing Tiffany in a big hug.

Tiffany returned it, even if she wasn't used to hugging people quite so freely and with such exuberance.

She always had to have a guard between her emotions and the people around her.

People who were too nice made her nervous and suspicious.

People like Miss Kendall.

Nice people normally weren't nice deep down inside, it was just a front they put on, to fool everyone around them.

Tiffany had seen more than one angry wife who was normally "nice" turn into a raging shrew, chasing her man out of the house and into the arms of a woman like Tiffany.

Mostly though, she just heard tales of what wives did behind closed doors, from husbands who'd walked away from those closed doors and found a woman who wouldn't criticize every word that came out of his mouth or every action he took.

Over the years though, she'd come to realize that those men really did love the women they talked about for the most part. Their frustration came from the fact that they didn't feel like those women loved them.

Not that any man ever articulated anything like that to her.

It's just what she'd figured out. Someone who spent as much time as she did with men had a tendency to notice things.

Men wanted to be respected and admired, not henpecked and criticized.

Even when the criticism came with a smile, it was still criticism.

"I thought you were going to get here earlier?" Leiklyn said when she pulled back.

"I did. And I'm sorry that I missed Willan for the day, but... I told you guys I was changing, and I decided I needed to do that first."

"You stopped at the church first, didn't you?" Leiklyn said with a knowing smile.

"I did."

"And Pastor Kane?" Leiklyn said, stopping just short of batting her lashes.

"He was there."

"Isn't he a godly man? So wise and sincere and just passionate about God and the things of God, and about helping people, and just tirelessly working for the greater good of mankind..."

"That's enough," Tiffany said, feeling bad for interrupting her friend but feeling like maybe her friend was laying it on just a little thick.

"Oh yes, and he's exactly your age. What a coincidence," Leiklyn said, and that time Tiffany was pretty sure she did bat her eyes.

"Mom," Trent said with an elbow on the front desk. "Is this the way girls always talk about guys?"

"No, it's just your mom," Tiffany said quickly.

"Of course it is. Do you think the girls talk about anything else?" Leiklyn said, giving Trent a wink, and he grinned up at her.

"I don't know who to believe. Or what."

"That's exactly what girls want you to feel. Confused," Tiffany said, exchanging a grin with Leiklyn.

"Then you're supposed to shrug your shoulders and walk away and think to yourself, 'I'll never understand women,'" Leiklyn said.

"What are you teaching that poor kid?" Ethan walked out into the hall and came to the front desk, stopping with his arms around Leiklyn and putting his cheek down next to hers.

It was such a sweet embrace, so familiar and so affectionate, that Tiffany looked away.

"I'm teaching him to stay far away from girls until he's old enough to be wise."

"You don't want him to get married until he's eighty?" Ethan said, and Tiffany bit back a snort. "Because that's about the time we get wise, isn't it?" Ethan continued.

"You're right as usual." Leiklyn sighed. "Eighty might be a little old, but sixty. We could go with sixty."

"Mom, you're not even sixty. I want to find a girl before I'm old enough to be dead," Trent said, half irritated, half amused.

"Don't worry about finding a girl, sweetheart. I'll find one for you. You just concentrate on your schoolwork and keep helping your dad with fixing up the inn."

"You just want a slave," Trent said, now sounding more irritated than amused.

"Pretty sure that's what women think men are," Ethan said, and then he shook his head as Leiklyn poked her elbow in his stomach. "I'm teasing, Trent. Your mom is right though, at your age, girls are interesting, but it's probably a good idea to stand back and figure yourself out before you try to attempt to figure out something as confusing as a woman."

"Am I really confusing?" Leiklyn said over her shoulder.

"Not normally. Perplexing, confounding, baffling. But not confusing. Not really," Ethan said, his arms tightening around his wife as she smiled and closed her eyes.

"Think I'll go out and shoot some hoops," Trent said. "You coming out, Dad?"

Tiffany was a little surprised at his use of the word dad, since Leiklyn was divorced from his biological dad, but she didn't miss the sweet smile that Ethan and Leiklyn shared nor the proud look that crossed Ethan's face. "Sure, son. I'd love to."

He dropped a kiss on his wife's forehead before his arm slipped from hers, lingering just a moment on her waist, then he followed his son out the door.

"I'm so happy for you," Tiffany said sincerely.

There was obviously some banter, and teasing, and a sweet spirit between the three of them, and it made her wish that she'd made different choices when she was younger. Choices that would have given her a loving husband and children that grew up to admire and respect her.

Instead, she was alone, desperately trying to atone for past sins, and almost penniless to boot.

"Thank you. You know there was a time in my life, right after my divorce, and various times while I was raising my children alone, that I didn't think I'd ever be happy. I didn't know what the point was other than living for my kids, because life just felt so hard." Leiklyn had a bit of a faraway look in her eyes, but then she shook her head and huffed out a breath. "But I learned through those years that you choose your own happiness, and you have to put the past behind you. It's over with, and all it does is eat you up if you let it."

"Your husband was a jerk. I admire you for saying you put it behind you. Is that true?" Tiffany asked, unsure how anyone could put the cheating of their husband and the breakup with their family behind them with no bitterness.

"It is. Because if I don't put that behind me, if I let that bother me, I'm not punishing him. I'm punishing myself. He doesn't give a flip whether I'm still angry at him or not. But my anger eats me. That's why forgiveness is so important."

Maybe no one ever explained it to her quite like that before, or maybe she just had refused to listen. But it made sense. Forgiving someone was less about letting them get away with it and more about freeing herself to not be bitter and angry and not allow those emotions to destroy her health and her peace of mind.

"My forgiveness needs to be pointed more directly at myself than anyone around me. I made a lot of stupid mistakes that hurt myself."

Tiffany moved the mouse pad so that it was exactly square on the low counter behind the high desk. Sure, her husbands hadn't always been completely kind to her, but she'd made bad decisions too. It really wasn't her marriages that haunted her, although they definitely had left her gun-shy when it came to men.

It was the things she'd done she had a hard time getting over.

That made it hard for her to believe that God had forgiven her. She could accept that, she just couldn't get over the guilty feeling and the regret, and the desire to go back and redo her life, being smarter than the first time.

"The same thing applies. Although, sometimes we want to punish ourselves, don't we?" Leiklyn shook her head and laughed a little. "We feel guilty, and so it almost makes us feel better to think that our guilt is hurting us, hurting our health, hurting our mental ability, but honestly, who wants to be miserable? You're not really helping anyone when you're in that state."

There she was, being wise again.

"I think that's why God gives us friends, isn't it?"

"What are you talking about?" Leiklyn said with a chuckle. "To make us feel guilty about ourselves? I hope not."

"No. Just to show us when we're being stupid."

"I didn't say anything about anybody being stupid," Leiklyn said, her eyes wide and innocent.

Leiklyn knew exactly how Tiffany felt about her mental abilities. She'd been called a bimbo, an airheaded cheerleader, and much worse in high school. Kids had made fun of and teased her for the stupid answers she'd given in class to the point where she'd stopped caring and laughed along with everyone else, pretending her dumbness was a joke.

Leiklyn would never call Tiffany stupid. Never.

"I know. I was saying that about myself."

"Stop it. You're not stupid. You're just smart in ways that a classroom can't measure."

"Really? And what ways are those?"

"You put clothes together and make things look gorgeous." Leiklyn ran her eyes over the baggy shirt and puffy pants Tiffany wore. "Except, today you apparently got up and went into somebody else's closet. What's with the outfit?"

"I sold most of my high-dollar stuff. I have a few bags left in the car that I figured I would donate to the secondhand store. I have a few things in a storage unit yet. Things I knew wouldn't get much at a consignment sale."

"You need to get those things back out and wear them. That's part of your gift. Knowing what looks good. Design, style. Those are gifts. Not everybody has that."

"It's a worthless gift. Design just draws eyes to you and sells your body like merchandise." She wanted to clasp a hand over her mouth, because her words had made Leiklyn's jaw drop.

But to her credit, Leiklyn didn't say anything, just shook her head. "It's not like that. There is a difference between making yourself look good, between being stylish and being trampy. You know the difference. I know you do. You've got that eye."

Leiklyn was right; she'd always had an artistic eye and a craftiness about her that was just natural.

"You also were quite artistic in high school." Leiklyn crossed her arms over her chest and gave Tiffany a look that dared her to contradict her.

She enjoyed doodling and drawing cartoonish figures, flowers, even a dog or person.

Kane's face floated into her head. If she doodled tonight, that's probably what would come out. Strong jaw, the manly stubble, the glint in his eye. She'd have trouble catching that glint, but she'd try, because that's what made his expression so appealing. His face was almost too handsome, but that glint turned it from hard to charming and approachable.

"I'd forgotten," she said honestly. She hadn't done anything but doodle for a long time.

"You should get an easel, some paints, chalks, or whatever, and get back into it."

"I'd hardly be a famous artist."

"You don't have to be a famous artist. But right here," Leiklyn lifted a hand and indicated the inn, "Indigo Inn sees all kinds of visitors. We'll put your artwork up in the hall, put price tags on it, price it crazy expensive so people think you're someone really amazing, and people would buy it. Souvenirs for their trip, or because they fall in love with one of your pictures."

"Do you think?"

"Of course. And you know, people with artistic brains, creative brains, they do terrible in classrooms, because everything is so structured. Following a certain set of rules is tough for their creative bent, and there's no room for coloring outside of the lines."

"But sometimes coloring outside the lines is where you get your best pictures."

"Exactly." Leiklyn nodded. "After all, God doesn't color inside the lines when he makes a sunset, does he? He just takes a big brush and paints the whole sky. Broad strokes, big and wide, sometimes even splashes it down on the lake and on the houses nearby. Whatever happens to be in the way gets hit with the beautiful colors, and he ends up with a masterpiece each and every night."

"I never thought of it quite that way, but you're right."

"Of course. That's what you need to do. Get yourself a canvas, maybe do watercolors or chalks. You've never done that before, have you?"

"I tinkered around with it a little bit in college. But not for more than a decade."

"Take your canvas out and be inspired. Sunsets over the lake are gorgeous. Absolutely stunning. You don't have to be here until eight o'clock, and at this time of year, the sunset is already over. You can take the early morning shift too, and then you'll get all of your hours in and still have time to paint."

They'd agreed that she'd work at least forty hours a week, and the inn would pay her. The inn was also providing a place for her to stay, since Ethan and Leiklyn had moved out of the cottage and into a home they'd bought not far away.

Leiklyn had explained that got them away from work, because when they stayed at the cottage, all they thought about was working on the inn, and they needed to focus on something besides work.

"Maybe I will."

"Let me just say, all teasing aside, if you sit in the parking lot of the church and you face the lake, it's a gorgeous view. If you're volunteering there, I'm sure Pastor Kane would let you hang out there in the evening and work on your painting. He really is a good man. And even if you two don't end up together, I know you'll be friends. You'll like him. Just give him a chance."

Tiffany nodded, thinking that she liked him too much. That was the problem. He wasn't the kind of man she wanted to be friends with. He was the kind of man she wanted to be more with, and she'd had enough of that kind of man to last a lifetime.

Plus, Pastor Kane wasn't exactly her type of man. He would be more than horrified if he knew her background and the things that she'd done.

"How long has he been pastoring here?"

"He was an assistant pastor for two years or so somewhere else, but I think he's been in Blueberry Beach about three years," Leiklyn said, moving her hands off the desk and shoving one in her pocket. "Why?"

"I was just wondering what he did before he moved here. Blueberry Beach is a pretty small town and a small ministry. You'd think he'd want to go somewhere big, somewhere where his ministry had the potential to grow into a mega-church."

"That's just it. He has the ability to do that, but that's not Pastor Kane. He's not looking at the money, and he's not looking at the prestige. He just wants to serve, and he said this is where God wants him, so this is where he is. You have to admire a man like that."

"I see." Tiffany's words were noncommittal, but she agreed with Leiklyn. A man who would give up the idea of a lot of fame, a big congregation, and a mega-church to hang out at Blueberry Beach was a man who was serious about his job and serious about the Lord.

It was the kind of pastor she wanted, if only she were looking at him as just a pastor and not with that annoying sense of attraction.

Regardless, she'd made a lot of decisions, and she'd stuck with all of them. She would simply decide that she wasn't going to feel anything for Pastor Kane, and she would stick with it.

Chapter 7

"THANK YOU, IVA MAY. You're looking chipper this morning," Pastor Kane said as he took his change from Iva May who stood behind the cash register at the Blueberry Café and stuck the coins in his pocket.

He usually left his wallet and all his cards behind when he walked in the morning, but thankfully most of the stores in Blueberry Beach, including the Blueberry Café, still dealt in cash.

"You're welcome, Pastor Kane." The older lady smiled, reminding him, as always, of Mrs. Claus.

Not that he believed in Santa Claus or even had strong feelings toward the man, considering that he was a pastor. If anything, Santa Claus sometimes distracted from the true meaning of Christmas, and he resented him at times.

Mrs. Claus on the other hand, if she were as sweet and nice as Iva May, might convince him to believe in fairy tales.

He wasn't sure why the idea of Mrs. Claus brought the image of Tiffany into his head, but it did.

What kind of woman would she be forty years from now? Thirty years from now?

Would she be smiling, with her eyes twinkling, a kind word for everyone, and a little wisdom to share with anyone who was interested?

Or would she be more like a sour, bitter old woman who held her Bible against her chest like a shield and wielded it like a club against anyone who dared to disagree with the doctrine she knew to be right as she turned up her nose and stormed away from anyone who didn't look or act like a proper Christian?

He knew plenty of old ladies like that. Some old men as well.

He hoped he didn't turn out like that. Not that sin should be winked at. Not that he felt that they should turn a blind eye to egregiously wicked behavior, either.

But it was the behavior that they needed to hate, because the command was clear to love the sinner.

He understood the idea that if a person who was sinning was ostracized from the group, it could make them see the folly of their ways and make them change.

He supposed there was a time and place for that. It was biblical, after all.

But Jesus taught a love that would draw people to him, by its very warmth and inclusiveness, and inspire them to change, to see their sin and wickedness and want to do better, not because they felt guilty and were doing penance, but because they loved Him and wanted to serve Him and be more like Him.

Sounded kind of far-fetched when he thought about it in his head, but he'd seen it happen in people's lives.

Knew it was possible.

Experienced it himself. God still worked that way, and he didn't want to be the kind of person that kept God from working because he was so busy judging everyone he forgot to love them first.

"When I grow up, I want to be just like you," he said to Iva May, who chuckled. Her cheeks got even redder, if that were possible, and she waved a hand at him.

"Go on, pastor. You're too young to flirt with this old lady. You go find someone young enough to appreciate your flattering words and then marry her quick. We need a pastor's wife."

"There aren't a whole lot of unmarried ladies in this town," Kane said, thinking that recently the town had just gotten one more, one he was very interested in, except...she was completely unsuited and totally unacceptable. Not for what she'd have to do and be as his wife.

"I know one," Miss Iva May said, reaching behind her and grabbing a cup for the coffee that he'd ordered.

"Well, there's this thing that happens," Kane said. "A funny little thing, that not only does she have to be my age and available, but she also has to like me in that way. People tend to look at their pastor and see spiritual things, not carnal."

"And that's the way it should be. You're a man of spiritual things."

But he was also a man. Just a man. He wanted the same things every other man wanted. Something to do with his hands. Worthwhile work that made him feel valued and appreciated. A family who admired and respected him. A wife who looked at him with adoration, who covered his weaknesses, made him look better than he did alone, gave him air, and helped him soar.

Not that he thought a wife was just someone to come along behind him blowing so he could look like a big shot. He wanted to be able to turn around and do the same for her. That together they were better than they were apart. That they looked after each other, and he protected and provided for her and gave her room to be creative and incredible in her own right.

There weren't too many women around who were interested in the biblical roles of men and women.

The world had taken something that was beautiful and right and twisted it, convincing a lot of minds that it wasn't the best thing. Funny, the same thing had happened when Eve was deceived with the fruit. Instead of having God's best, she ended up with less.

He couldn't be a one-man show to try to right that wrong though.

Knowing that didn't keep him from longing for it. Didn't keep a lot of men from longing for what they were made to crave, made to need, what they required in order to be complete.

"Pastor?" Iva May asked, uncertainly, the napkins she'd been trying to hand him still hovering in the air as he gazed unseeing at them.

"I'm sorry." He reached up and took the napkins.

"It's okay. I know you're probably looking for someone to see you as more than just a spiritual leader. Miss Kendall speaks very highly of you, and while she's a bit younger than you, you two have a lot of interests in common." Iva May smiled sweetly, and then her head turned as the bell jingled and another customer walked in.

"You're right. She's a nice lady, and I like her." All true, but not exactly what Iva May might think.

Miss Kendall didn't make his heart race. Didn't inspire him to gaze into her eyes and fight the totally inappropriate desire to spend every waking second with her. Her image didn't pop into his brain before he went to bed at night and wasn't there when he woke up in the morning.

Every night for the last week, he had had an image in his head. For the first time in a long time.

It was still there in the morning as well.

He waved again at Iva May as he walked out of the diner, coffee cup in hand, steam coming out the little hole at the top.

He walked down the sidewalk, the cool fall wind rustling leaves and dead grass around his feet.

Nodding to Bill at the surf shop, he continued on down past the Little People Shop and the hardware store, nodding to the man who was outside sweeping.

Wishing he had worn a beanie hat to go along with his jacket, he squared his shoulders against the wind and kept walking toward the church. It was up on a little rise, not quite overlooking the town, and angled so that the view out the big picture windows in front took in Lake Michigan.

A gorgeous place for church, and he'd fallen in love with it the first time he'd seen it.

Although of course, he hadn't come to be the pastor because he'd fallen in love with the location of the church.

He'd come because he knew this was where God wanted him.

Lord, send someone to labor with me.

He supposed it shouldn't have surprised him when, three hours later, while he was kneeling at the altar, he heard the vestibule doors swing.

He finished his sentence, told the good Lord he'd get back with Him in a bit, and raised his head to see Tiffany standing in the back.

He pushed to his feet and turned. She didn't move.

"This is the second time I've interrupted you in that position. Is that all you do all day?" she asked, and while the words could have been taken sarcastically, that wasn't her tone.

"Kind of funny that I have a job where I get paid to pray," he said, wondering why he couldn't think of anything better to say. Just looking at her seemed to have stolen his words. Not good, if she was going to be showing up here at the church every Monday, since it had been a week since she'd last been there.

She'd been in the congregation yesterday, paying close attention to his sermon, but she'd left without speaking to him.

"That sounds easy, except, when I go to pray, I end up thinking about everything in my life except the things I need to pray about."

"I still have trouble concentrating sometimes, even though I've gotten better at focusing on just having a conversation with God. That's really what it is. Sometimes, it's being quiet listening to Him talk to you."

"I thought that's what the Bible was for?"

"Sure. It is. But prayer too. God doesn't want us to have a one-sided conversation with Him."

"How do you know it's God talking and not yourself thinking it?"

"Good question. I guess it's kind of one of the reasons I know the Bible is true. If I were going to write a Bible, a history of my people, I sure wouldn't have made up a history like the Israelites have. Where they're constantly rebelling, constantly not believing, constantly turning to idolatry, constantly doing all the things they're not supposed to do. I wouldn't have David commit adultery. I wouldn't have Jacob steal his brother's birthright. I wouldn't have Eve eating the apple."

"It's always the woman's fault," she said and rolled her eyes. But her face was interested; she was listening.

He kept going like she hadn't interrupted. "I wouldn't have had Judas betraying God's son, and I wouldn't have Stephen stoned. I could go on and on. There's just so much junk in the Bible that wouldn't be there if I were writing the story. Or if anyone were just making the story up and trying to say that they were God, you know? God just puts it there and shows men the way they are. Sinful and hopeless. Helpless without Him. And He doesn't need to say that, although He does, because He shows us."

She had a thoughtful look on her face like she hadn't considered all the things that he was saying before, but then she tilted her head. "I don't understand what that has to do with hearing what God has to say to you."

"Well, if I'm doing the thinking for myself, I'm thinking the things I want to think, right? I think things that are convenient to me. Things I want to know, or want to do, or want to hear. Not that God doesn't speak those things to me, but... Sometimes He says the hard things too. For example, I was just complaining to Him this morning about something, and when I was done complaining, He said to me, *if I thought you needed that, I would have given it to you. But since I didn't, maybe you should stop whining about what you don't have and start appreciating what you do.*"

"God said you're whining?"

"Okay, so that's a little bit of a paraphrase. I think He might have spoken in a little bit gentler way, but yeah, sometimes we need our wake-up call."

"I see." Then she looked around the church. "Well, I'm here to volunteer. What are we doing today?"

He laughed, even though he tried not to. He just couldn't help it.

Most of the time, he had to lasso people, hog-tie them, and give them a tranquilizer before they were willing to do anything in the church.

Here was this woman, who didn't know up from down when it came to Christianity, who was here begging to help.

"What?" she asked. "What's so funny?"

He shook his head. He couldn't explain it. She wouldn't get it, hadn't been in church long enough to understand.

She crossed her arms over her chest and got a bit of an offended look on her face.

He put a hand up. "I'm not laughing at you. I promise. It's just... It's just sometimes...most of the time...really hard to get church members to volunteer for anything. Oh, there's some who volunteer for everything, but we say in church all the time that ten percent of the people do ninety percent of the work. And it's true. And here you are, practically begging me to do something, and I don't have anything."

"You weren't going to do anything today?"

"I was going pray. And study my Bible. Work on some sermon notes."

"That's it?"

"Those are pretty important things. Prayer changes things, and how can I shepherd my flock if I'm not in God's word, studying and reading and feeding myself?"

She seemed like she understood that, and her chiseled chin lost its jutting-out position. "So I need to find something to do myself?" She looked around the sanctuary, as if a job was going to jump out of the corner somewhere.

"Miss Kendall has told me over and over again that if anyone is available, they can come and read a Bible story to the children, but most of them are in school now."

"The ones that aren't don't understand. There's no point," Tiffany said dismissively.

"Oh. That's not true at all. Children are very impressionable when they're young. In fact, the Bible says *train up a child in the way he should go, and when he is old, he will not depart from it.* Some people say if you have a child until they're six, you have their heart for the rest of their life."

He liked that she didn't come off disagreeing with him right away but thought about things first. Like now, her face scrunched up, and she seemed to be considering what he said.

Pretty soon, she nodded. "I don't know if that's entirely true, but I guess it is accurate. You kind of feel like you're born with a certain knowledge, but it's actually what was instilled in you at your home, whether it was by your parents, whoever watched you, or what you figured out for yourself."

"That's why it's so important for children to have stable homes. Good influences. For people to care and not just leave their kids unattended as long as they're being quite good." He thought for a second and then decided, since she was here, he might as well take advantage of it. Sometimes people got really excited about being a Christian, ready to jump into everything, and sometimes those people burned out, disappeared from church, and never came back.

He probably shouldn't let good help go to waste.

"I told Zoriah, who owns the secondhand store, that I would spend some time in the back separating donations and seeing if there was anything there that would work for our missionaries. She donates a good bit to the church rummage sale, every year, and in return, I usually try to donate some time to helping her out. Would you be interested?"

He almost didn't ask that last question, because it was obvious from the way her eyes lit up and the smile on her face that she was more than interested.

Even though her clothes looked rather old and baggy, she seemed like the kind of woman who would have good taste and a flair for fashion.

"I have some sizes, children, adult, man and woman, for our different missionary families, and I'll grab those from my desk on our way out."

"Sounds great. If you have the sizes, I can fix nice clothes up for them. I actually have some in the trunk of my car that I've been meaning to donate anyway. We can go through those too."

"You carry around clothes in the back of your car?" he asked, knowing that wasn't the case but curious about her. Wanting to know more. Odd, because he didn't typically have that problem.

She was shaking her head but also smiling. "No. I cleaned out my closets, sold what I could, and figured I would donate the rest. That life is behind me, and I'm not going back. I might as well change my dress as well as my life, right?"

He eyed what she was wearing, baggy slacks and a frumpy sweater. He hadn't noticed until just that second that her hair was braided and tied just above her shoulders.

It didn't look like she wore any makeup at all, and her coat was army green, unbuttoned in the front. In fact, it might have been missing buttons.

"Well, the sentiment is correct. When you choose Christ, it means you turn your back on your previous life, on your sin. That's what repentance is, and it's a necessary precursor for salvation. But it doesn't mean that you have to give up things that weren't wrong to begin with. Like your clothes."

"You haven't seen my clothes," she said with a warning look.

"Okay. I admit I know nothing about fashion or women's clothes, so you could be right."

"I know I'm right," she said, walking with him and waiting at the door of his office while he walked in and rooted through his desk drawer until he had the piece of paper that he'd jotted the sizes on.

"So you're not up with the digital age?" she asked.

"The sizes came in email, but they came in five separate emails, so I wrote them down, figuring that I would eventually need them all in one spot. I suppose I could have printed off five emails, but it seemed like a waste."

"Oh. So we're looking for more than just one family?"

"Yes. The church supports more than five missionaries, but these are the ones who responded when I asked if they had a need for clothes. There are some particulars on here as well. This one family specifically asked for jeans and winter items, while this other one is asking for girls' skirts." He waved the paper around, and she took it out of his hand, skimming through what he'd scratched down.

As she squinted, he wished he had taken time to write a little bit neater, but at the time, he'd figured it would just be him going through it.

Honestly, he hadn't been looking forward to it. Picking out clothes was not something he enjoyed. He spent as little time as possible on his own, let alone trying to find some for someone else.

"I see a couple of sizes that will work with the clothes I have in the back of my car." She held the paper with one hand and tapped her chin with her other finger, sighing. "I don't have a whole lot of things that will probably work for missionaries but some tops and a few bottoms. If we can't find the rest of the stuff going through the secondhand shop in Blueberry Beach, there are more shops around, plus I know people who know people." She smiled in a way that made him think she would do whatever it took to make sure the list was filled, correctly and quickly.

"I separated them here. That's what these lines are for, to show which clothes go with which families."

"I see. What you're saying is I can't throw all these clothes in one bag or box because they're not all going to the same place?"

"That's right."

"Perfect." She started striding out of the church, pushing open the back door. She stopped when she realized he wasn't behind her.

She turned, lifting a brow at him. "Are you coming?"

He wanted to. For the first time in his life, he wanted to go clothes shopping, or whatever it was called, because he was absolutely sure he would have fun with her, but... He knew he shouldn't.

He needed to stay away from her. She was too tempting. Too much like someone he wanted to be with, and she was all wrong for him.

Not to mention, despite her baggy clothes, he got the feeling she came from an upper-crust background.

She would be horrified to learn his.

"You actually seem like you might have that in hand. Would you be offended if I just let you loose, and I don't go along? I stink at shopping anyway." He held up both hands and hoped he hadn't offended her.

Who was he kidding? She was probably relieved he wouldn't be there, bumbling and in the way. In his experience, when women shopped, a man's place was usually on the periphery, ducking to keep from getting hit by flying apparel.

Maybe it was his imagination, but she looked disappointed.

"Of course not. I can handle this easy peasy. In fact, this is *so* up my alley."

"I can see it is." He forced himself not to sound disappointed. Taking another breath, he said, "I might run over and see Miss Kendall. Now that you're here and enjoying this, she might have some kids that need some clothes, and I'll get some sizes and information from her. Obviously, you're good at it, so why let your talent go to waste?"

His words didn't make her as happy as what he thought they would. He figured she'd be beaming at the idea of more shopping, but if anything, her face seemed to fall.

"Yeah. Why let it go to waste. I'm so glad we found something that I'm good at." Her words were the right words, but her expression seemed stiff. Maybe that was the plastic surgery. Not that he would know, but he nodded, and she waved the paper before turning and walking out the door.

He felt like a teenager, because he wanted to run after her. Wanted to go with her. Just for any excuse to be beside her.

She was all wrong for him, and he needed to figure out how he could convince himself of that.

He also needed to figure out how he was going to be able to work with her if she was going to continue to show up at the church and ask for things to do. He needed to give her jobs that would take her away from him.

This was perfect, and he should thank the Lord for the inspiration, should ask for more ideas, because he was tempted to try to think of things that they could do together.

And that was the worst thing he could do.

Chapter 8

TIFFANY HAD NEVER FELT like pouting so much in her life before.

At one point in her twenties, she pouted a lot.

It never did any good, so she broke the habit. She'd rather be strong and decisive than whiny and whimpering anyway.

But today, she wanted to cross her arms over her chest and stomp away, annoyed.

But she didn't. Obviously. She was an adult, and she was changing anyway.

With God's help, she was changing. It was way too hard for her to do it on her own.

But there's so much about God she didn't know.

Just in ten minutes today, Kane had taught her more than she'd learned in the last six months on her own.

She spent the short walk into town and down the sidewalk getting a hold of herself.

He was right to send her away to do this by herself. Of course he was. There was no need for him to go rooting through clothes with her when she could do it perfectly fine on her own.

There was no need for her to be offended or upset.

It just made her feel like he didn't want her. Which was ridiculous. Not that he didn't want her, but that she was upset about it.

He was absolutely reasonable in saying that he didn't want to go shopping. What man did?

She almost knocked on the door, then came to herself and shook her head. She needed to be paying attention and quit walking around in a daze.

Walking into the store, she smiled when "Jingle Bells" played. It was still fall, but "Jingle Bells" made her smile.

Blueberry Beach was an amazing town. She was staying. She was going to be in Blueberry Beach, she was putting down roots, she was volunteering, she was creating a new life for herself.

"Good morning," a kind voice said as a figure stood from a rack toward the back. "Is there something in particular I can direct you toward or are you just browsing today?" The lady wore a long flowing skirt and comfy-looking sweater and seemed to flow toward her.

"Actually, I'm here on behalf of Pastor Kane. I have a list of sizes and clothes that he would like to have picked out for the missionaries?"

"Oh, yes. He mentioned that he'd be down. I think that was like three months ago." The lady laughed, and she sounded like she'd be a fun person to have a conversation with. "He doesn't like to shop." She leaned in and said that close, like it was a secret.

Tiffany shrugged, but she leaned forward and said back in the exact same tone, "What man does?"

See? It wasn't a personal thing.

Normally, she didn't have trouble with confidence, but maybe it was her clothes and the fact that she felt like she didn't have her normal armor on. Whatever. She was over it.

"I'm Zoriah, and I don't think I've seen you around before. That's why I thought you were a customer."

"I am Tiffany," Tiffany said, taking the slender hand that was proffered and meeting Zoriah's eyes as she shook it. "And I'm new in town. I have a one-third interest in the Indigo Inn, and I'm planning on staying."

"Oh! I vaguely remember you and your friends from our high school years. I was with my gram a lot during the summer. She used to own this shop."

"Zoriah! I remember now. I'm so sorry. I didn't recognize you. I heard you moved away, and it never even occurred to me that you'd be in your grandmother's shop."

"Honestly, it wasn't something that I had ever thought of either. It's just the way the Lord works things out sometimes."

"He certainly does things that I don't understand, I admit."

"Let me show you to the back, and you can see the things that we just got in first and you can take anything there you need."

"Aren't those the things that you're going to sell?"

"They are," Zoriah said. "But Pastor Kane always makes a huge contribution that more than pays for what he takes. I tell him to use the money for something else, but he insists. So, of course I give him anything that he wants, and he gets first pick if he's fast enough. But I can't let stuff sit back here for three months, so he missed out on some."

"If I'm around, he won't miss out on much anymore. If that's the way it really goes. Does the church really donate that much money?" That felt like a gossipy question, but it seemed like one that she should be able to ask if she were going to be a part of the church. She should know what they did with their finances, right?

"The church does well. There are some people in town with money. A couple of doctors, and a few other people associated with the hospital. Not a whole lot of people know, since she does most of her donating anonymously, but Beverly—you might remember her, she grew up in town, although she's much older than we are—amassed a big fortune and then semiretired. She's back in town a good bit and donated for the children's cancer wing at the hospital. She also donated the money to start the children's home that Miss Kendall runs. If you're hanging out with Pastor Kane, I'm sure you'll meet Miss Kendall." Zoriah leaned forward, like she was sharing a secret again. "I think Miss Kendall and

Pastor Kane are perfect for each other. I'm not sure they've realized it yet, but the town kind of has this thing going where we keep trying to matchmake, so now that you're in on it, you can jump on any opportunities to push the two of them together." She winked and straightened back up.

"Thanks. I appreciate being included." Tiffany tried to inject enthusiasm into her words, but it was tough. She wasn't even sure why. Miss Kendall was a sweet, Godly woman who was selflessly doing good in the world. Pastor Kane deserved the best.

Miss Kendall was perfect and much better for Kane than Tiffany. Plus, she'd just met the man a week ago.

But this odd feeling she had when she was around him, not just attraction, although she felt that for sure. But more like rightness. Like a comfortable feeling that made her feel content, despite the prickling sensation that hovered in the back of her neck when she was around him.

It had only been a couple of times. Maybe it would go away.

"All right, follow me and I'll show you where you can start."

"Wait. I have clothes in my car to donate, although I didn't get this list until after I had them packed up, and I think I have some things I can use for it. Can I bring them in and go through them in the back along with everything else?"

"Sure," Zoriah said. "I'll go out with you and bring those on in. We'll just walk through the store right now."

"I can give you help with that," a deep voice said, startling Tiffany. She turned her head. A tall man, handsome with intelligent eyes stepped out of the back and walked over to Zoriah. Putting his arm around her, he leaned down and pressed his lips against her temple.

She leaned into him, and Tiffany got the same feeling from watching them that she got from watching Leiklyn and Ethan.

It was super sweet and nice to watch two people who were obviously in love be with each other.

But it was also discouraging. She'd been married three times and never had anything close to what they had.

The idea of a fourth marriage was repugnant.

The idea of actually finding something that special seemed totally out of reach, like a daydream or fairy tale.

"This is my husband, Gage," Zoriah said, smiling with her arm wrapped around his waist, hugging him close. "Gage, this is Tiffany." She looked up at her husband. "She's new in town, and she's here for Pastor Kane, but she has some clothes in her car to donate first."

"That's what I was giving a hand with," Gage said, humor in his voice.

"I left it right out front when I walked up to the church." Tiffany turned and walked out the door, smiling again as "Jingle Bells" played above her.

She hadn't even noticed the displays in the window until she was going back out, but they were cute, too. One of a bunch of people ice-skating, and another with a bunch of sledders sliding down a snow-covered hill.

She popped her trunk, and Gage came around, taking all the bags but two. Zoriah and she grabbed those.

Gage held the door, and they walked to the back of the shop, past racks of clothing, some antiques, shelves of books, and a few electronics. There was some furniture scattered around the periphery, and kitchenware as well.

"You have a bit of everything," Tiffany said as they walked through the doorway into the back room.

"We do. Growing up, if you remember, my grandmother just had apparel. It just didn't work out when I first came here, although that's what I was originally going to do. I'm so glad it didn't, because I'm really loving this. Every day, you never know what's going to come in, just interesting stuff, and a lot of times, people bring it in with a story."

"It's hard to find good help anymore. The help I've got likes to talk to the customers rather than selling stuff to them," Gage said, smiling fondly at his wife.

"I'm in charge of customer relations."

"Oh? Is that what that's called?"

"It is. Now get back to work." She did a shooing motion with her hand. Both of them were teasing, and Tiffany felt like she might have stepped into a private joke.

It was sweet, to see them laughing and having fun with each other.

It was a marriage like she'd never seen before. Not growing up, and none of her own.

"Nice to meet you, Tiffany," Gage said as he lifted a hand and walked out.

"Does he work here, too?" Tiffany asked as Zoriah adjusted the bags and turned around.

"He does. It turned out that shortly before we got married, he lost his job. He does a lot of buying and selling online, and during the spring and summer, we're often busy going to yard sales and cleaning out storage containers, people's attics, and even whole houses." Her eyes lit up as she talked. It was obvious she loved what she did and loved being able to work with her husband. "We're always busy, too busy, probably, but my niece and nephew, who are like my children, help out when they can, although he's in school right now, and she's away at college."

"I love it. A family business. It sounds wonderful."

"It is. More wonderful than I could have ever imagined. I never dreamed that my life would turn out like this. So much better than I expected." She smiled, her eyes glowing, her movements graceful and sure as she moved around, adjusting a couple of racks and moving a few boxes.

"Here are all of the new things. I have some things hung up on racks, as you can see. I've a tendency to organize them by size and of course gender. If I can't tell, I just use my best judgment." She smiled and lifted a hand like what else could she do. "If you don't mind, I'll work a little bit alongside of you, doing some sorting, while you go through figuring things out."

"I don't mind at all." It was true. Zoriah was such a sweet and genuine person Tiffany almost totally forgot her distrust of kind people.

Zoriah took a few minutes to get settled, and they got into a rhythm with their work before Zoriah broke the comfortable silence that had fallen between them.

"So you're working for the church?"

"No. I'm working at the Indigo Inn. I own one third of it, and I'm the only one that hasn't been doing anything. When we decided to come back and open it, it took me a while to get my loose ends wrapped up. But I'm here now and ready to pull my weight."

"It's pretty amazing how quickly they've been able to get the inn fixed up and open. And customers just rave about it." She folded one shirt and set it on the pile, then grabbed a hanger for a second. "It used to be this time of year was completely dead, but with the inn, we have a steady trickle of customers all fall. It's been a real benefit to us."

"I'm so happy to hear that. I know my friends will be too."

"Oh, they know. Trust me, we make sure to tell them."

"They said the town has helped them a good bit with getting the inn fixed up. They've had several town-wide workdays. They're so grateful."

"That's just the kind of town it is. It wouldn't be Blueberry Beach without that pulling-together spirit. So you're working for the inn and volunteering at the church?"

"That's right. Although, I just started volunteering last week. I've never actually done it before, and maybe I was a little pushy to begin with. I think Pastor Kane was scrambling to find something for me to do."

"Why do you say that?"

"Well, I walked into the church and asked to volunteer, and he seemed a little flabbergasted."

"Yeah. I don't think he normally has people beating the doors down to help. I'm sure he appreciated it."

"Maybe he will, once he gets used to it, but for now, I think, like I said, he was scrambling to find things for me to do."

She folded another pair of child's jeans, size six, and put them in the pile she had started for that missionary family.

"Looks like he found a job you're good at. It's really fantastic, too, because when Pastor Kane had to come in and do this, he hated every second. He did it with a smile, but you could tell that he'd rather be watching sand drain out of an hourglass than sitting in here looking at tags on clothing and trying to pick out stuff that worked for the missionaries."

Tiffany laughed. "Well, this is right up my alley. I just love this kind of thing. I love shopping, love clothes, love fashion, love trying things on and feeling like a princess."

"Oh, me too. Even you saying that brings back memories of my grandmother and just growing up in her shop and spending rainy afternoons and snowy days playing dress-up."

"Funny how that's something girls love and boys can't seem to stand."

"Little boys in particular can't stand it. I remember when my nephew was little, and he absolutely hated to change his clothes. But my niece would have on five or six different outfits every day if she was allowed."

"Just funny how that works."

"Girls and boys are so different. It's kind of crazy that we try to pretend they're not."

Tiffany had never really thought about it like that, but she supposed it was true. They really were different.

"Different, not necessarily better or worse," she said as the thought came into her head.

"Of course. Everyone has their different abilities, and you do what you're good at. When it comes to a family, moms are designed for certain things, and dads are designed for certain things. Not necessarily things we like, but it's the way God designed it."

Tiffany nodded, because it all made sense.

Chapter 9

TIFFANY HAD MADE IT through the first bag and started into the second. Her last husband had children from a previous marriage, and she had packed up some of their clothes, glad now that she had. They hadn't been around her much but had been at their home long enough to have an entire wardrobe of things in each of their rooms.

"So why are you so forceful about volunteering? Is it a passion of yours?"

Tiffany didn't want to talk about that. She'd have to talk about her past, and the things that she'd done, and things she didn't want to admit to anyone or have anyone know about. So she didn't say much, just, "Yeah. It's a good thing, right?"

"Sure is. I bet if you give Pastor Kane a few more days, he'll have all kinds of things thought of for you, and you'll be busier than you know what to do with. When do you work at the inn?"

Tiffany told her her schedule, and they chatted for a while with Tiffany managing to get through a second entire bag before "Jingle Bells" chimed in the room, and Zoriah looked up.

"Excuse me." She straightened from the pile of clothes she had been bending over. "I'll see if this customer needs help, and then I'll be back."

"Take your time, I'm fine here." Tiffany said, enjoying the company but fine working by herself as well.

She didn't really pay attention and so was startled when Zoriah said, "She's right here. Of course you're welcome to help."

There were some footsteps, and then a familiar voice said, "Hey, there. How'd you make out?"

Kane stood in the doorway, tall, with broad shoulders that she didn't associate with a preacher, and if she were guessing, she would say he looked a little sheepish. Like he was slightly embarrassed that he was showing up when for all intents and purposes, he told her he wanted her to do it herself.

"Is there a problem?" she asked.

Had she done something wrong? She had been in the church for a few minutes and hadn't touched anything while she was there, other than taking the paper in his hand from him.

"No. Nothing's wrong. I just... I just figured I'd come help you."

"You hate doing this. You have to be ecstatic that you found someone who would do it for you," Zoriah said in disbelief.

"I know. You'd think," he said, kind of enigmatically, and Tiffany wasn't quite sure what to make of that.

"Jingle Bells" started playing, and another customer walked in.

"If you'll excuse me," Zoriah said. "Pastor Kane, you know you're welcome to anything."

"Thanks, Zoriah," Kane said, coming in. "Is it gonna bother you if I'm here?" he asked, after Zoriah had walked out.

He took another step into the room, making it feel like the walls were closing in and the air was being sucked out.

It was just her imagination. She had to own it.

"It's fine, of course. I'm just a little surprised because you seemed adamant that I was doing it by myself."

"I know." He didn't say anything more, and she was disappointed. She wanted to know why he'd come. What had changed his mind? "Can I see the list, and I'll start looking for something in particular if you want."

He wasn't going to say anything more, wasn't going to tell her why he'd decided to come back.

So she put her finger on the list, showed him the things he could look for, all the while wondering if he'd decided that she needed to be supervised. Did he think she was going to steal something? Was he concerned that she might not get along with Zoriah? Didn't he trust her?

She kept her mouth closed for a few minutes while he started digging through some piles of clothes.

His movements were jerky, and she was pretty sure he put at least two pairs of pants aside that wouldn't work, and she almost laughed.

But she didn't, because there were tons of things she wasn't good at, and last Monday was a case in point. He hadn't laughed at her when she didn't know what to say at the hospital with the patient suffering from dementia, and he hadn't laughed at her when she'd gone to the children's home and felt uncomfortable.

It would be rude for her to laugh.

But eventually, she couldn't take the suspense anymore, and she said, "I thought you were going to the children's home. Was Miss Kendall away?"

"No," he said and didn't say anything else.

She picked out another top, a perfect size and a conservative pattern. She folded it, setting it down carefully before she said slowly, "I thought pastors were supposed to be a little bit more personable?"

"Huh?" he said, his head snapping around, his eyes narrowed. "What do you mean?"

"You've just been answering all my questions with monosyllables."

"You have a thing against one-syllable words?" he asked, looking back at the clothes in front of him.

"Not at all. I love one-syllable words. However, typically when one answers a question, unless it's a yes or no question, one answers with a sentence. Not a monosyllable. Although I suppose it's rude of me to mention it, because it sounds an awful lot like complaining."

"No. You're right. You're not complaining, you're being truthful." Kane's hands stopped moving, and she noticed for the first time that they were a little rough, a little brown, slightly calloused, and not necessarily the kind of hands that she would expect to see on a preacher.

Her eyes got caught on his fingers, and she watched as they moved across the fabric, turning the tag, and holding it while he read it, then turning it back and folding the shirt up.

"I'm sorry. I'll try to do better." He took a breath. "You're right. I was going to go to the children's home, but I decided to come here instead. And I guess the reason I answered you with a monosyllable is because I don't really know why I changed my mind. And I kinda feel like I shouldn't have, and I'm annoyed with myself about it. So that's why I was short."

"I thought maybe you didn't trust me, and you feel like you need to come back to supervise me. Like I was going to steal something or be unkind to Zoriah."

"No!" he said immediately, jerking his head up and twisting to look at her. Then he deflated a little. Like he knew his reaction had been over the top. "No. That's not it at all. Far from it. In fact, you might not be the typical type of person who darkens the door of the church, but there's something about you that makes me think I can trust you. Maybe that's wrong, but I don't think so. Typically, my gut is right, although I don't always go with it."

"That's more a woman thing, isn't it? Woman's intuition," she said, folding a skirt and for the first time losing track of which pile was which.

She was way more into him than she should be when he could distract her so easily. She'd always been serious about clothing and loved organizing as well. She should be able to do this in her sleep.

"So, since we are in here together, and you're upset with me for being monosyllabic, how about you tell me what you did before you moved to Blueberry Beach and I'll listen to you, and I'll learn how I should talk."

Oh boy. He'd asked her the last question she wanted to answer, then almost challenged her not to answer it by telling her to do better than what he had done.

"Maybe it's my turn to be monosyllabic," she said, buying time, because she wasn't sure what to say, scrambling to say something that was true but not the whole truth. She definitely didn't want to give him the whole truth.

"You're supposed to be the good example here, show me what's right. Teach me to talk. Isn't that what men need?"

"You're a pastor, although that might be a good thing, if you need to be taught to talk, that must mean your sermons aren't very long. Right?"

She looked over and looking at the side of his face could see his grin. He didn't look over but was smiling down at his hands.

"You can say that if you want to, but when you come to church on Sunday, you'd better pack a lunch."

"Wow. I've never heard that one before."

"I said lunch not supper, so don't get too scared."

"So I'm packing two fish and five loaves of bread, and you're feeding the entire congregation?"

"I talk about Jesus, I'm not him." But then he mumbled, "Sometimes people get confused."

"Really?" she said, just as though he'd meant to tell her that and she was replying.

Maybe he wouldn't answer, especially since he hadn't been planning on saying it, but he nodded. "Yeah. At least in the sense that they think I should be perfect. Maybe not perform miracles exactly, although people come to me and talk about their kids that are in deep sin, and they want me to somehow fix it. The time to fix it was when they were little and cute and nobody wanted to discipline them. Once they're old and have decided to do their own thing, there's not much I can do. It breaks my heart regardless. I always try, but the results aren't usually good."

He paused while folding a pair of jeans. "I'm not blaming the parents. Sometimes things happen. Sometimes people just make bad decisions that lead to more and more bad decisions."

"I was one of those kids that thought they knew better than all the things that they'd been taught when they were kids, and I went off and did my own thing." She figured she could talk in generalities, and he wouldn't know exactly how terrible she'd been. "Which of course my own thing was a lot of things that I knew I shouldn't do but thought were good ideas anyway. Nothing turned out right. I was a miserable failure for most of my adult life so far, which is why I came back to Blueberry Beach and which is why I showed up at the church wanting to volunteer. I have a lot of paying to do for the sins I've committed."

"You do know that you don't need to pay for your sins. It's already been done."

"Yes, I know. I understand the theology, I just... I just feel like that wasn't enough. Like in order for me to show that I'm truly repentant, I have to pay."

"Then you don't have faith that Jesus's payment was enough, right? If you still feel like there's something to pay."

That stopped her cold.

She stared at the little girl's pink fluffy skirt in her hand and barely saw it.

"I never thought about it like that," she finally said, a slight amount of wonder in her voice.

Was that true? If she still thought that she needed to pay for what she'd done, then obviously she actually believed Jesus's payment wasn't enough? That had to be right if she felt she had to make up for things somehow?

"I think a lot of people don't. I know this might shock you, but I have some things in my past that I'm ashamed of."

"It does. Everyone I've talked to in Blueberry Beach thinks you're a saint."

"They didn't know me ten years ago. Or they would never say that. And I don't typically talk about that too much, because some people are pretty judgmental. Thankfully, God is the righteous judge, but He's not judgmental. When Jesus paid the price, he paid it all. When we accept it as an individual, there isn't anything left for us to pay."

"But... But why do you do good things then? Isn't that to make your good things weigh more than your bad things?"

He grunted, and then he said, "Not at all. There is no such thing as making your good things weigh more than your bad things. There is no way that your good could ever outweigh your bad. It's just not possible. Or maybe I should say it's not possible for your good to ever be good enough. Because your good will never be holy, and that's God's standard—holiness. So you can try all you want to, but your good works won't get you anywhere, and neither will mine."

"But I don't get it. What's the point of good works then?" She was starting to get agitated. He was knocking everything she thought; although she had believed that Christ's work on the cross was enough, she just also believed that she needed to work to be good enough.

"I guess if you didn't have good parents, maybe it's kind of hard to understand. And sometimes you can see it in your children. But just pretend you have kids that you love. Do you want them to listen to you and obey you because they feel like they have to? Because they're paying you back for something? Or do you want them to do kind things to you because they want to? I guess you could say that about friends or anyone. You don't want people to be nice to you because they have to. It's drudgery, but they do it anyway because they have to." He said that with a certain amount of flair, and she smiled as he acted like he might be imitating someone that was whining about the work they had to do.

"You're right. I... I guess there's a lot I have to learn. Because I wasn't thinking like that at all, but I can totally see what you're saying. God wants us to serve Him, not because we have to, or because we have to meet a certain standard, but because we want to."

"That's right. Same thing's true about dress, or about modesty, or even about traditional gender roles, or anything else you do as a Christian. Loving your neighbor, loving God. Going to church. God doesn't want you to get up in the morning and go it's Sunday and then grumble grumble grumble your way to church. He wants you to get up and go with a cheerful heart, grateful you have the opportunity, thankful that you get to spend a little time with Him and with other Christians. See the difference?"

"So easy to see the difference when you're explaining it to me. But I'm guessing tonight when I'm alone, I'll start trying to validate my need to work to be good enough."

"Well, don't get me wrong, because God calls us to holiness. After all, He wants us to be like Jesus, and Jesus was sinless. But He wants us to do it because we love Him, not because we have to. Although, that standard is impossible."

"Then why try for it?"

"Because we're supposed to constantly want to get better. And I do. But in my own power, I can't do it. I need to remember that everything I want, everything I want to be, comes from God. My very breath. I couldn't take another without Him. I can't sustain my life at all. Think about it. What are you doing to keep yourself alive?"

Again, he was right. He'd been right about everything.

She laughed. "I didn't wake up this morning and give one thought to whether or not I need to keep myself alive. I didn't even think about waking up, come to think about it. It just all happened."

"Exactly. And you can believe that's chance, which a lot of people do, or you can believe that there is a loving Creator, sustaining your every breath, keeping you, and loving you. And that's the thing. God loves us more than we can ever know."

"I don't understand how He could love me." She didn't want to say more. She didn't want Kane to think so much less of her, although she was curious as to exactly what was in his past that he had been hinting about that the people in Blueberry Beach didn't know. "I was so terrible."

"It doesn't matter how terrible you are. Even though He's holy and can't stand sin, He loves you with a love that you can't even comprehend. As in, the same way we don't understand the universe, we can't comprehend how big it is, we don't know what's in it, and we don't know how those things work...oh, sure, we can guess, but we don't know. That's the same way it is with God's love. We don't understand it, we can't really see it, we have no idea of its depth and power, and we won't, not in this world."

Honestly when she'd started doing the clothes, and Kane had walked in, she hadn't thought she'd be getting another theology lesson, but she needed it. She had needed to hear that she wasn't supposed to be throwing herself into the work, pushing to do whatever she could, trying to make up for what she'd done.

It was a relief to know that she could do it because she loved God, not because she felt guilty.

"I guess I'm giving you my sermon for Sunday. I'm sorry. You wanted me to talk, and you know I'm a man, so I'm going to talk shop."

She laughed. "Theology is shoptalk for you. I'll keep that in mind." She hadn't minded. Not at all. In fact, he made her feel a lot better.

"Just to prove I can do it, let's talk about something else. You pick the subject this time."

"I think I picked the subject last time. At least, I don't think it was just you going off. I was interested," she added, almost defiantly, because she had been interested. Truly.

But he was determined and started talking about Christmas, and the decorations the town put up every year, and how the lake looked in December, and pretty soon she was laughing and adding to the conversation, because after all, she grew up in Blueberry Beach, and she could tell him where he was wrong and what had changed over the years.

It ended up being a very pleasant morning.

Chapter 10

NOVEMBER HAD COME AND almost gone.

Kane hunched his shoulders against the wind. As the sun had disappeared beyond the horizon, chilliness had descended. Still, Tiffany sat at her easel in front of the church.

She'd helped serve their Thanksgiving meal, although she wouldn't have anything to do with cooking it. She'd scrubbed every dish and hadn't rested until the tables were wiped and the floor swept and everything put away.

He had a lot of hard workers in his church, but he'd never seen one who worked like Tiffany.

Still, he thought that their conversation of almost a month ago had changed her attitude, and instead of seeming desperate to atone, she almost seemed like she was cheerfully serving.

Maybe that was his wishful thinking, since they hadn't spoken about it again.

They'd fallen into a routine, where she came every Monday morning after he'd had his devotions and prayer time, and possibly made a couple phone calls, and done a little studying.

They often visited the children's home, she'd cleaned every inch of the church, sometimes they entertained kids dropped off by the bus or visited a new family who had moved in.

Whatever he had on the agenda, she did.

He couldn't tell her no when she'd ask if she could sit in the church parking lot each evening as the sun went down.

She couldn't have known it was his favorite time of day, and he loved nothing more than to stand in the sanctuary in front of the big window and watch as day and night did their daily dance, twisting and moving and shimmering until day finally bowed gracefully out, and night took over.

The whole performance was enchanting, magical, and he never failed to think of the Creator and his infinite creativity in having every single day be completely different than the day before, even if there were similarities.

How something could be completely different and yet so much the same, he couldn't answer. But it awed him and thrilled him, too.

And now almost every night, Tiffany sat in front of him.

Eventually, the cold wind from Lake Michigan would have to drive her inside until spring.

Part of him dreaded it. Part of him looked forward to it. He already spent at least eight hours with her every Monday. Sometimes, she came another day during the week. He didn't need her to be part of each magical twilight as well.

It was almost full dark, and she had started packing up her things.

Occasionally, he went out and helped her, but he didn't want her to know that he watched her each evening. If he went out every night just as she was cleaning up, surely she would start to get suspicious.

So instead, he went to his office and sat down. His Bible was open on the desk, and he leaned his head over it.

Lord, I want to look at her all the time, I can't stop thinking about her, I make excuses to spend more time with her. You have her here. You brought me to Blueberry Beach, you brought her to my church, begging to help. What am I supposed to do?

"Knock knock?" Tiffany's voice broke into his prayer as she tapped on the doorframe.

She never came into his office, and he appreciated that. It wasn't exactly his sanctuary, and they would never have the door closed behind them, but he felt like a man in his position could never be too careful.

"You all finished?" he asked, rhetorically, since she obviously was, considering she was holding her canvas and her easel along with the paints.

"I am. I was wondering if you had a minute where you could come down and look at this mural that I've been working on in the teen room?"

More, Lord?

He smiled and nodded, pushing up from his chair and waiting while she put her things in the copy room closet.

She'd gotten comfortable in the church in the month that she'd been there, and people had accepted her without question. Especially when she was willing to do whatever anyone asked, including singing in the choir, even though she insisted she wasn't that great of a singer, and she didn't know most songs.

He'd refrained from rolling his eyes when the choir director said, "If you don't know the song, just sing softly."

He'd wanted to say how that kind of defeated the purpose of having her in the choir, but he didn't, because he was just happy to have someone who was willing to do anything.

"You're quiet," she said as she led the way down the stairs.

"Thinking," he replied, figuring not in a million years would he tell her what he was thinking about. Although he believed in praising people, and complimenting them, and giving them credit where it was due, he couldn't do that with her.

Couldn't do that without her knowing how he truly felt.

She led the way to the teen room, flipping on the light, walking in, and saying, "Ta-da!"

He promised her he wouldn't be in the room until she finished it, and it hadn't been a hard promise to keep. Adam and Lindy Coates taught the teens each Sunday, and he had no need to be down here.

"Wow," he said, looking over the flat Michigan landscape, blueberry plants hanging thick and ripe, full dark blue against green, touched with the dew of the evening, the sun setting in the background over the lake, shimmering, and somehow she caught the dance. That dance of light and dark, and even though the painting was not heavy, a person standing looking at it could still tell the night was coming. Still see the subtle entwining. The mixing and the shimmering and the invisible waves twisting together.

"Is that wow in a good way, or wow in a I can't believe this is in the teen room and how am I going to find a color dark enough so I can paint over it way?" she asked, her voice uncertain.

"It's a wow as in you're incredible way," he said, remembering too late that he couldn't give her compliments.

But she smiled, pleased, and looked back at the wall. "It took long enough."

"As big as it is, it should have taken a while. Even if you hadn't caught everything that you did in it, just the sheer size of it would have taken a long time."

"I work on it almost every afternoon for at least three or four hours."

"Time well spent. That's unbelievable. You have a real talent." He looked at her as he spoke, and her eyes looked pleased, but then they widened slightly as they roved over his face.

Maybe she could see what he was thinking, what he felt, what he wanted.

He just hadn't decided whether it was the right thing or not.

Sometimes God answered clearly, and he knew beyond a shadow of doubt what he was supposed to do. Like moving to Blueberry Beach. Like becoming a pastor. Like supporting the children's center, and even knowing which message to preach on Sunday. Normally, God was quite clear.

But his feelings got in the way when it came to Tiffany, and he couldn't tell where what he wanted stopped and where what God wanted started.

"Do you really think so?" she asked, and while there was hesitation in her voice, there was also pleasure and maybe a little bit of admiration, like she was glad to please someone she admired.

He didn't need her admiring him. It was one of the last things he needed.

But it was there in her eyes, and he couldn't look away.

He wanted to walk toward her, close the distance, touch her. All three of those things were a bad idea.

Still, he wasn't exactly thinking about that as he took first one step, then two, and then his hand reached out and touched her cheek, running one finger down the cool softness.

Her breath hitched, but he barely noticed since his own heart and lungs were not cooperating at all. His heart had somehow taken the place of his stomach, which felt like it had fallen at his feet.

"You are beautiful," he murmured, running his thumb over her cheekbone but not necessarily talking about the physical attributes he was looking at. Rather, the person as a whole. Because of who she was, because of what she was, because of everything that made her up, all the things that were unseen, she was beautiful to him.

There was way too much emotion in his voice, way too much everything.

But he couldn't back away, couldn't stop touching her, couldn't stop wanting her to touch him.

The words to ask, or maybe demand, that she do so trembled on the tip of his tongue, but she didn't need them. Her hand was already moving, landing just below his rib cage. Her touch soft, gentle.

Knowing he shouldn't, his head started moving down, and he didn't even try to stop.

Their breath mingled, and he breathed in her air. Her eyes fluttered and closed, then his did too.

"Oh! I'm so sorry. Wow. I'll just go upstairs and wait."

Kane jerked back. He didn't mean to, but the voice had startled him. His hand dropped, and Tiffany stepped back as well. They both stared toward the door where Miss Kendall stood with her hand to her throat before she whirled around and practically ran down the hall toward the stairs.

"Miss Kendall. Wait."

His voice was completely different, commanding and somewhat lower, loud, and even Miss Kendall, in her flight, listened, almost screeching to a stop.

"Come back here," he commanded.

Now that the spell had been broken, he realized he'd made a huge error in judgment, a major mistake.

He slowly turned his head and looked at the woman he'd almost kissed.

Yeah. There was hurt in her eyes. Confusion, too. Both of which slowly gave way to anger as her eyes narrowed and her arms crossed over her chest.

But then a smile, plastic and insincere, pulled her lips up.

Yeah. He'd been a jerk. He'd almost kissed her, and she knew it, and then he'd jerked back like a teenager caught shoplifting. Now he just called another woman back rather than explaining and apologizing to the one in front of him. The one he really wanted.

Still, the damage was done, and Miss Kendall stood in the doorway again.

"Really, I would rather wait upstairs," she said, her voice devoid of emotion and her eyes flat.

"I'm sorry," he said, looking at Miss Kendall but knowing the words should be directed at Tiffany instead. "I'm sure that wasn't what you were expecting to see when you came down here."

"No. It wasn't. I wouldn't have come down if I'd known you two were... But I was looking for you because I had a favor to ask of both of you." Miss Kendall's kindly eyes went from him to Tiffany, who didn't look very happy, but he knew the anger was justified from the hurt he'd inflicted, and that he couldn't do anything about.

"What is it?" Tiffany asked, no longer looking at him, and her smile seemed to melt into something that looked sincere.

He deserved that, too, since he'd treated her so badly.

"I was hoping you two would be able to watch the kids for me next Monday. I need to go home because my mom is having a procedure. While I'm there we were going to do some Christmas shopping, and meet friends, and I was going to do all of that in one day, but Becky, you know the lady who helps me, is going home for Christmas early, and she won't be there. The kids are really good, and usually one person would be fine, but I would be more comfortable with two."

Kane struggled to put his pastor persona back on. He'd just gotten caught doing something that no pastor should ever do, and Miss Kendall was kind enough to overlook it and still ask him to do what she'd come for.

Maybe that meant she wasn't going to tell anyone, but he didn't want to bank on that. He needed to confess or at least own it.

"I'd be happy to help you out. Tiffany?" he asked, and his tone had been completely businesslike until he'd said her name, and somehow it just curled off. Even he could hear the notes of affection, of wanting, of admiration.

He couldn't take it back, nor did he really want to. A man couldn't trust his feelings; so many times, people got into trouble because they thought their feelings were true when they really weren't. Feelings came and feelings went; it was what the person had put their trust in rather than God.

But the fact was he was falling for Tiffany, and he was very close to not caring who knew it.

"I would love to," Tiffany said, sounding sincere. He believed she was. She loved to help. That hadn't changed. "If you're going to be gone past 8 o'clock, you'll have to let me know so that I can find someone to take my place at the front desk at the Indigo Inn."

"I think it would be a good idea. It will be late before I get back."

"That's fine," Tiffany said. "I'll find someone."

"What time would you like us to be there?" Kane asked.

"As early as you can make it. I'll have a long drive ahead of me, and I'd like to get started."

They settled on a time, and Miss Kendall thanked them and turned to go.

"Miss Kendall?" Kane said, and she stopped, lifting inquiring eyes to his face.

"Yes?"

He swallowed. His throat was tight, and his mouth wanted to move up and down, flopping with no words. He gritted his jaw. "I'm not sure how Tiffany feels about me, but what you walked in on was sincere on my part, and honest."

Miss Kendall put her hand up. "Please stop. I was actually here be-cause I've seen you two together when you've been at the children's home, and just the way you look at each other, the banter between you, the way you both seem to know what the other's thinking, what they're going to do, and the way you look out for each other. Just different things like that." She lifted her shoulder. "It's made me think that there's maybe more than friendship between you. Although, I feel like neither one of you know it." Her smile was a little crafty as she said, "I feel like the whole town has been conspiring to get you and I together," she looked directly at Kane, "so I decided it was okay for me to do a little matchmaking of my own. It's possible that I might have scheduled the day I need to be away for the exact date that Becky wouldn't be there, and I would need to ask two people to sit and watch the children. And it's possible that the romantic in me decided that you two would be the perfect choice to spend the day together. Forgive me."

Kane's mouth hung open. He couldn't help it. He wasn't thinking about his mouth or anything, other than glancing at Tiffany to see if she was as shocked as he was.

If possible, her mouth hung open wider than his.

"And as for what was happening in here when I came down, I truly didn't mean to interrupt, but it didn't shock me. Whatever is between you two is between you two. No one will hear anything from me about it." She gave them both a smile, genuine and happy, before she waved a couple of fingers, turned on one boot, and walked out of the room. Her footsteps faded as they went up the stairs, and the silence of the room pressed down.

It was time for another apology. The important one.

"I'm so sorry," he said after he turned to face Tiffany.

She wouldn't look at him. Although she'd gotten her mouth closed, the expression on her face was anything but happy.

"I shouldn't have jerked back like we were guilty of some kind of mortal sin. I was surprised, but truth be told, that wasn't really the way I had wanted our relationship to go."

"Stop. It's fine. You and I would never work anyway. So everything was for the best." She looked everywhere but his face, her hands fiddling with her jacket, pulling it down, and tugging on her gloves. "I better get going. I'll be late for my job. I'm glad you like the mural." Her words were short and clipped, and her movements jerky.

She started toward the door.

"Tiffany. Wait."

"No. It's fine. That wasn't the way I wanted our relationship to go either, truth be told," she said, mimicking his words with one of her plastic smiles as she swept out of the room. Practically running.

He almost called her back, but it typically wasn't in his nature to be commanding, and he'd already done far more of that than he was comfortable with this evening.

Plus, she was right, she was going to be late.

He watched her go, wishing he could do the last half hour over again.

If she's not the one, Lord, please show me, because I'm afraid it's almost too late.

He'd barely spoken the words when he realized the Lord might possibly show him that she wasn't the one for him by having her not return his feelings.

The thought was painful.

Chapter 11

"AND I THINK HE ALMOST kissed me."

Iva May nodded, sitting behind the front desk with Tiffany, the rest of the hotel silent and dark.

Asleep.

Only the tiny light at the top of the desk gave a glow to the downstairs. It was well past midnight, and normally Tiffany would be considering leaving, but Iva May had come around eight o'clock, sat down, and they'd been talking about how the town had changed over the years, and different ideas for next year's Blueberry Festival, and discussing the new Christmas decorations the town was considering buying and how much they loved the old ones.

Tiffany wasn't exactly sure how they'd gotten onto the subject of Kane, except somehow she found herself admitting that he was on her mind constantly, and she knew she wasn't good enough for him. Wasn't cut out to be a pastor's wife.

For sure.

Wasn't spiritual enough to be a pastor's wife.

Iva May had mostly been nodding and listening, but finally, when Tiffany confessed what had taken place in the teen room earlier in the evening, and Miss Kendall walking in, and how Tiffany was afraid that any budding romance between Kane and Miss Kendall had been ruined by her, because Kane had almost kissed her, Miss Iva May finally spoke.

"And would that have been a bad thing?"

"Of course! Haven't you been listening to me?" she cried. "He's a pastor. He's almost perfect. He's everything that I'm not. I can't have him kissing me. And it's even worse because the person that he's supposed to be kissing walked in on us."

"But you said that she said she was matchmaking between you two. It sounds to me like she doesn't want to kiss him."

"Miss Iva May. You know how women are. She was probably just saying that to save face. The whole town has been trying to get them together, and she knows it. And yet there he is almost kissing me. What else was she supposed to say?"

"Did it ever occur to you that if the entire town was trying to get them together, and she knew it, and they still weren't together... Maybe they weren't meant to be together."

"Oh wow." Tiffany stared at her hands clasped tightly in her lap. Could Miss Iva May maybe be right about that?

"Sometimes our brains trick us into believing the worst-case scenario. Sometimes we look at people and see only the bad. Assign bad motivations, the worst. And most of the time, it's just a lie. It's a lie that we convince ourselves we need to believe."

"I know." She'd caught herself doing that more than once. Assuming the person who cut her off in traffic did it on purpose and forgetting that she constantly cut people off, just because she was a bad driver and not because she had it out for anyone behind her.

So many times, people didn't mean to do the unkind things that they did, but it was hard to remember that and give people the benefit of the doubt, as she would want for herself.

"It's all about what we do to others, really, when it boils down to it," Miss Iva May said.

"I know. If I want other people to think the best of me, I need to think the best of them. How do you feel about going to the children's home and watching the kids for the day with Pastor Kane?" she asked hopefully. "I could take your job at the cash register at the diner if you have to work."

Hopefully, the pleading in her tone wasn't too noticeable.

Iva May shook her head, a smile on her face, determination in her eyes. "You can't run from this."

"If I don't run from it, I'm going to have to tell him what I was. And that will make him run. And it will be easier if I do the running."

"Easier isn't necessarily better," Miss Iva May said, her hands clasped across her stomach, leaning back in her chair, her eyes tired.

"You're right. I've kept you up way too long. I think it's time for us to go."

"I'm old, and you're right I'm tired, but I'm never too old, never too tired to talk."

"I appreciate it. I guess I never really had a mom to talk to, one who would give me good advice anyway. Maybe that's why the Lord never gave me children. Because I would have been a terrible mom."

"From what I hear, you're excellent with the children. The boys come in the diner, and I hear snatches," Miss Iva May said.

"The diner is a really great place to keep up with everything in town."

"It sure is." The smile on Iva May's face faded a little, and she said, "I feel guilty though, because I've definitely counseled you to tell your secret. But I have one too. And I know it's rude of me to tell you I have a secret without planning on telling you what it is, but I can't. Still, I've been putting it off long enough, and I need to tell people before it's too late."

"Too late?"

"Nobody lives forever, honey."

"Are you saying that because you know you are going to die soon, or because everyone dies?"

"Mostly the second." Her hand came over and settled on Tiffany's leg. "I have a doctor's appointment in a month, but I just have a feeling."

"Get rid of the feeling, stop it. I need you," Tiffany said, and her panic was real. Since she'd come to Blueberry Beach, Iva May had been a rock for her. Tonight was the first night that she'd really confided much, but every time she'd talked to Iva May, she felt like she was gleaning wisdom. She needed Iva May.

Why did God seem to take people just when they were needed most?

"If you need me, I'll be here if I can. But that's for the Lord to decide now, isn't it?"

"I know you're right, but I don't have to like it."

"That's true, you don't."

Tiffany was just getting ready to suggest that they leave again when the door opened.

They did have a room, several in fact, as they'd just gotten two finished this week, but as late as it was, Tiffany couldn't stop the churning of her stomach until she saw that their guest was a woman.

Blueberry Beach was safe. A great town with small-town vibes, but one could never be too careful.

"Good evening, and welcome to Indigo Inn," Tiffany said, standing as the woman approached the desk.

"Good evening. Do you have a room?"

"We do. Just one?"

The woman nodded. Her voice was a little harsh, the kind of harshness when someone was afraid, deeply scared. "Do you know where the owner of the inn is?" she asked, then immediately shook her head. "Never mind. It's late. She's probably sleeping."

"Well, I'm one of the three owners. The other two are at home with their families." Tiffany tapped a few keys on the keyboard, and the computer sprang to life. She looked back up at the guest. "Do you need me to call them?" She cringed inside as she asked. If it were an emergency, she most definitely would call either Willan or Leiklyn. But she didn't want to wake them up if she didn't have to.

But the woman's tired eyes, fear oozing out of them, snapped open as they landed on Iva May. "You! You were in the room that day." She said the words like an accusation, and Tiffany moved closer to Iva May, unsure of what exactly the woman was getting at but knowing that she needed to protect her friend.

Iva May stood slowly. "You're the woman whose husband left her," she said quietly.

"Yes!" the woman said. "I need to talk to you. I've tried everything, done everything that I know of to do, and nothing has worked. I've begged him on my knees, begged him to take me back, and he agreed to have a trial reconciliation." She swallowed, and her voice grew hoarser. "It didn't work, and he says he just can't take it anymore. I dismissed everything you all said that day, but I'm willing to try anything. No one else will tell me what will work. I need to know."

Iva May nodded. "Are you staying here tonight regardless?" she asked gently.

The lady nodded. "Yes. I told him I would give him time to cool off, and then he agreed one more time to a mediator, but the divorce is drawn up. The papers are ready. All we have to do is sign." Her voice broke, and she took a moment to compose herself. "I don't want to lose him. He's a good man. He truly is, but I've driven him to this, and I don't even know how."

"I think half the battle is admitting that you are part of the problem," Iva May said softly. "Does he say he still loves you?"

"He says he wants to, but I've made it hard. And I honestly think he would have come back and allowed me to come back and stay, but...I think he looks at our kids and doesn't want my example. Like I'm pushing them away from him, and so help me, I think he's right!"

"Let's talk in the morning." Iva May patted her arm, her face wreathed in sympathy. "I think you'll feel better. You'll be rested, better able to listen and think, and you can go home with some things that could potentially save your marriage."

The lady gripped Iva May's hand, and to Tiffany's surprise, she felt her own hand being gripped as well.

She covered that hand with her other hand, driven to give comfort, even though she had no idea what to say to the woman.

"I can't guarantee anything, but your husband was a reasonable man and a good one. You can fix this."

"I hope so. I've insisted for so long that it's all his fault, that he's the one that needs to see reason, I'm not sure that he's going to believe me when I tell him I finally figured out it was me."

"He'll believe you when he sees the changes."

Tiffany finished getting the information for the woman's room, and she pulled her credit card out with trembling fingers. After Tiffany had run it and asked Selena to follow her, she said to Iva May, "Will you be here when I come back down?"

"I can be. It's about time for this old lady to get to bed."

"I'll walk you home."

"You don't need to."

"I want to. I have a couple things I need to ask you."

Iva May nodded, and Tiffany fought to not be impatient as she showed the lady her room and explained that there would be baked goods and fruit on the buffet in the morning.

True to her word, Iva May was waiting when Tiffany came back down the stairs, her hat and coat on, waiting by the door.

Tiffany grabbed her things and shoved into them before opening the door and closing it softly behind them.

The night was crisp and cool, the breeze from the lake chilly, as they stepped out onto the sandy trail that led to the town. It was a short walk and an easy one, especially with the moon at three quarters lighting most of their way.

"What in the world are you going to say to her? Why are you so sure that she can fix her marriage?"

Iva May let out a slow breath, fogging up the air around them. "You weren't here when she burst into the sunroom a couple of months ago. She wanted advice, but mostly she just wanted us to tell her that she was right and her husband was wrong, then she wanted someone to go to him and talk some sense into him and demand that he take her back."

"And did you?"

"No. We didn't tell her what she wanted to hear. We told her, gently, what she *needed* to hear. She didn't want to hear it."

"How did you know what she needed to hear?"

"She'd been around the inn. Different people had heard her, and... Well, let me just say this. Nobody could do anything to please her. If the ceiling was red, she wanted it to be purple. Actually, let me be more specific, her husband couldn't please her. No matter what he did. If he walked right, she wanted him to walk left. And she didn't hesitate to tell him. And even if she said it in a kind way, a person, especially a man, can only take so much of that constant correction, the snide remarks, the acting like she's put out when she doesn't get exactly what she wants, before he can't take it anymore. I'm not saying her husband was right to leave or to insist that she needed to, but he wasn't the one who was asking for advice, it was her."

"I see."

"If you're going to be a pastor's wife, people will want counsel. It might be a good idea for you to sit in tomorrow. Whichever way it goes. I know last time she wasn't very interested in hearing us."

"Sounds like it's going to be different this time... Wait. Pastor's wife? I thought we decided I'm no good for him."

"And here I thought we decided you were going to tell him your secret," Iva May said as they stopped in front of the door of her house.

Tiffany laughed. "I think you're being obtuse on purpose."

"And I think that's you," Iva May said. Her voice held humor.

"I guess the bottom line is I'm scared."

"That's probably the bottom line for all of us. Now, do something about it." Iva May gave her a hug, squeezing extra tight, and Tiffany just wanted to lose herself in the warm embrace.

But Iva May was right. There came a time in a person's life when they had to stand up and do the right thing. She supposed this was her time.

Chapter 12

KANE DABBED A SMALL bit of glue on the shower tile he held in his hand before carefully turning around and pressing it against the wall next to the three tiles he'd already placed on the bottom row.

Doing shower tiles was exacting work and one that took a good deal of concentration, especially to get started.

If the bottom row wasn't square, the entire thing would be completely crooked—obviously crooked—by the time he was finished.

It was the kind of job he needed right now.

Behind him, Dr. John Chambers was putting the same kind of tile, slightly smaller and in a slightly different pattern, above the sink.

Kane made sure the tile was square, pressing it in.

He and Dr. John had already talked about the weather, Dr. John's daughter, and the fact that Dr. John and his wife had another baby on the way.

They'd lapsed into silence, which Kane was completely comfortable with, since he felt like he had a lot to think about.

Pastor Stuart, the man who was usually his mentor, was on a mission trip, or he would have called him last night.

He wasn't exactly ashamed of being caught almost kissing Tiffany in the church, and he certainly wasn't afraid of Miss Kendall telling everyone about it.

He hadn't been doing anything wrong, even if it probably was behavior that most people didn't expect their pastor to engage in.

The problem was he wasn't sure whether he should pursue a relationship with Tiffany, or whether it was just him wanting something God didn't want him to have.

"So all we've done so far today's talk about me. My kids, my wife, and I think I even threw in a few baby tips there. They were free by the way," Dr. John said after a few minutes of comfortable silence.

Kane paused with the glue in one hand and a tile in the other. "It's a good thing. Pastors don't make a lot, and I can't afford much advice on my salary."

"I cut way back from the big salaries and everything that went along with them. In fact, I would say there are a lot more important things in life than making a lot of money. My family being the main one."

"That's good. So many men are confused about what's important. It's refreshing to talk to someone who knows the value of the people in his life."

"I know I'm blessed to have Anitra and our little girl. Soon to be two little girls."

It was obvious that John was super proud of his family, and honestly that made Kane happy. The church, the country, and the world in general needed more men like John. People who were willing to sacrifice whatever it took to be a good husband and father.

Of course, it helped if a man found a good woman. One who was willing to stand beside him, one who would build him up instead of tearing him down, one who was equally willing to do whatever it took to keep her marriage together and to love her husband and support him.

Maybe there was no such woman for him.

Maybe because of his past, he'd lost the opportunity that God had for him to find someone.

"What about you? Is there a reason you've never married?" John asked, his question casual, his attention focused on the tile in front of him.

Kane kept his sigh from being audible but still blew his breath out, wondering how much to say.

A pastor had to be careful. He couldn't treat the people in his congregation like his best friends. Best friends knew way too much about each other to want to listen to a sermon by one of them on Sunday morning.

That's why he usually counseled with Pastor Stuart.

Dr. John was a professional and a doctor, and he'd seen more than his share of life and suffering. John was a godly man, who would give him advice based on what the Bible said and not what was currently popular in the world.

"If I'm being too nosy, you can say so," John said, breaking the silence that had fallen when Kane didn't say anything.

"No. I just...I don't know how much to say. I'm kind of struggling with something, and I was really thinking about how to present it so that it doesn't make me sound too terrible."

"Well, don't let the doctor title fool you. I could say lots of things that I've done that would make me look awful."

"I guess that's reassuring," Kane said dryly.

Dr. John laughed. "There are lots of reasons why people might not want to get married. And don't feel like you have to talk to me about them."

"It's not that I don't want to. It's that I'm sure about what God wants me to do with my life. I know I'm meant to be a preacher." Kane picked up a tile and flipped it over, ready for the glue. "And I know I'm meant to be here in Blueberry Beach. That's as obvious to me as anything. God clearly showed me those things." He paused with the glue brush in his hand. "But... I'd really like a wife. I've talked to the Lord about it a good bit, and I told him I'd wait until he brought the person he wants for me. I didn't have to rush ahead and just pick anyone. I'm willing to marry whoever God wants me to. In fact, that's the only person I want. The person God has for me."

"That sounds great. In fact, there's nothing I can say to that. If God has someone for you, that should be the only person you consider. I think the problem with a lot of people is they go with their feelings and whoever looks good. And that's probably a bad way to pick a wife." He paused for just a moment. "I'm just as guilty of that as anyone, only the Lord worked it out for the best."

"You were married before Anitra?"

"No. But our relationship definitely started out based on feelings. Still, there was always something about her that felt different. That felt like she wasn't the same as every other girl, but I'm not gonna lie and pretend I knew when I laid eyes on her that she was the one that God had for me."

"That's just it. I found someone who feels like that to me. But again, I'm dealing with feelings. When I look at facts, she doesn't look like a pastor's wife, she doesn't act like a pastor's wife, and I'm not even sure she wants to be a pastor's wife. And in my profession, I really need a woman who wants to be part of my job and what I do. People will expect it, and not that we have to give people everything that they want, but I want that, too."

John was silent, carefully setting a tile, and Kane considered that maybe he'd said too much.

Finally, John stepped back and looked at his handiwork, then grabbed another tile before saying, "Did you ever consider that sometimes the way we expect God to work isn't the way He does?"

Kane paused, the ache in his knee as he knelt on the hard floor forgotten as he considered what John had just said.

"I mean, how many times have we asked the Lord for something and he answers our prayer, only the answer that we get isn't the answer that we were expecting to see. Or it's not in the way men see it." He laughed and threw a hand in the air as though saying *look at this*. "Actually, Jesus is a prime example of that. People were looking for a king. They were looking for a Messiah. They were looking for someone to come with pomp and circumstance and riches and glory, and God had Jesus come to earth and make his appearance in a cattle stable. Know what I mean?"

"Yeah. I guess I don't really understand what the point is, though."

"You said that the girl that you're thinking of, and I'm just gonna take a wild stab at this and assume you're talking about Tiffany."

Kane grunted. "I wasn't very subtle about it, was I?"

"No. And you're right, she doesn't look like a pastor's wife. But sometimes the way people look isn't what we should be using as our yardstick. For instance, take Saul. He was head and shoulders above everyone else, tall in stature and handsome, and everyone thought he would be the perfect king. But it turned out he was a terrible king. And David, who was the youngest of eight, and he wasn't even considered important enough to come to dinner to eat with Samuel, he was the one that God chose as king, and he made one of the best kings the world has ever known. God calls him a man after His own heart. So I guess my point is, again, sometimes we ask God for something, a wife for example, and yet we're expecting a certain kind of person to walk into our lives. And that's where we're expecting our answer. We don't realize God has the answer sitting right in front of us, and we can't see it because it doesn't meet our expectations or look like what we expected the answer to be."

"I see." It was like light had dawned across the sky. Like dawn when the sun rose and did that dance with the darkness only this time the light won and the darkness went away.

Is that true, Lord? Is Tiffany the one, and I've been too blind to see it?

"So you think that Tiffany would make a good pastor's wife?" Maybe he shouldn't have asked like that. He was just begging for an insult to Tiffany, and he wished he wouldn't have uttered the words, but it was too late. They hung in the air, and he didn't want to pull them back in.

"I think whoever God has for the position will be the best pastor's wife that our church could possibly have. I think someone who went to sixteen different Bible colleges, and grew up as a child of missionaries in Africa, and was surrounded by Christians all their life, won't make a better pastor's wife than Tiffany, if she's the one that God wants you to marry."

His words made complete and total sense, and Kane was kicking himself for not thinking that earlier. Although, he wanted to hear what he wanted, and he was afraid to believe the truth.

"I guess I know that, I just... I just know that I want her, and sometimes we have a tendency to make what we want God's will for our lives. I've done it before and had disastrous consequences."

"I know. I've manipulated my life into thinking I'm doing what God wants when I knew deep in my heart that I was just pleasing myself. It's an easy trap to fall into."

"Right. Which is why I wanted to be careful."

The bottom row was finished, and it was exactly even with the plumb line he'd put up. He picked up another tile.

"What's it gonna take for you to decide that you need to move forward with Tiffany? Maybe she's not even interested. Have you considered that?"

Dr. John looked over his shoulder, and Kane looked up and met his eyes.

"Yeah. All these hurdles. All these things have to work out for us to work out. I guess I just need God to be clear. But I don't know exactly what that means. It's not like He's gonna make the sundial go back ten degrees or have the dew fall everywhere except my fleece. I think He's gonna be a little more subtle for me."

"I wouldn't be so sure. Sometimes, God can really knock us up alongside the head to get our attention."

"True."

"Knock knock?" a voice said, and that's all it took for Kane's heart rate to double.

Tiffany was in the doorway.

He looked over his shoulder and raised a brow. A woman he didn't recognize was standing with her.

"Pastor Kane, would you have a few minutes to speak with us, please?"

She called him Pastor Kane. That felt weird. He thought they were at least on a first-name basis. Maybe she was doing it for the benefit of the woman beside her.

"I do. Let me stick this last tile on before the glue dries, and I'll be right with you."

"All right, if you don't mind, we'll just go to the room across the hall. It's empty and unfinished."

"I'll be right over."

"Pastor Kane?" John said once Tiffany had left. "That's a little formal. Maybe you need to worry whether or not the woman's interested in you."

"Yeah, that struck me as a little odd too." He didn't figure there was any point in explaining that she might have just been showing respect in front of a stranger. He hoped that was it.

He stuck the tile on and rinsed his hands off, taking his kneepads off and shoving his phone in his pocket just in case he needed his Bible app.

Then he walked across the hall.

Chapter 13

TIFFANY STOOD WITH Selena, trying not to act nervous.

Iva May had texted earlier and said she hadn't been able to leave the diner, because it was Dr. John's day off and she didn't have anyone to cover for her.

That would have been fine if Willan and Leiklyn had been there. But Leiklyn had texted her saying that Trent had a cold and she was going to keep him at home, and Willan was going with Myla to her six-week postpartum checkup.

Everyone had thought someone else would be able to work the desk at the inn, and to be fair, Tiffany was the only one scheduled.

Regardless, she wasn't qualified to counsel anyone, so she did the only thing she could think of and went and got Kane.

"I don't want him to tell me the same thing that everybody else has been telling me. I want him to tell me what the ladies were saying when I talked to them before. Something about me, what I need to do."

Selena paced back and forth, obviously still as anxious and upset this morning as she had been last night.

If she'd slept at all, Tiffany couldn't tell. Her eyes were bloodshot, with dark circles around them, and her clothes hung on her body.

Obviously, she'd gotten to the point where she was willing to do anything.

Sometimes, people had to get to that point before they would change.

Tiffany could definitely commiserate with that.

"Good morning, ladies," Kane's voice said from the doorway. "What can I do for you?" he asked as he shut the door behind him.

"Do you want me to leave?" Tiffany asked, looking at Selena.

"No," Kane said before Selena could say anything.

"If you don't mind, I would prefer you stay as well," Selena said, sounding almost humble and a little scared.

Tiffany nodded, a little scared herself honestly, although she wasn't sure why.

"Pastor, I need you to help me." Selena folded her hands together and took a step toward Kane.

"I will if I can," Pastor Kane said gently, looking around. "There are a couple of buckets of spackling over there. How about we sit down?" It was a question, a suggestion, but he walked toward them, and Tiffany followed him, figuring that if he wanted them to sit, she would sit. Selena didn't say anything but followed them over, sitting down as well. Pastor Kane arranged his bucket so that it was slightly closer to Tiffany.

Had he done that on purpose? She wasn't sure, but she almost felt like it was him and her facing Selena.

"Okay. Let's start again. What's the trouble?"

"My husband left me. I was convinced it was his fault. I was convinced that people needed to go to him and convince him he had messed up and he needed to fix himself and come back to me. That didn't work." Selena's lips pressed together, like she was frustrated with herself, and it took her a bit to start talking again, like she had to collect her thoughts. "And so I came back to the only people who were willing to tell me what I needed to do." A ghost of a smile, albeit a bitter smile, crossed her face. "I guess everyone's scared of me. I wouldn't know why."

Tiffany did not snort.

Kane's face did not change.

Selena looked a little guilty, but she plowed ahead. "When I'd come here, asking for the ladies to help me, they were willing to, but they wanted me to do the changing. Apparently, they saw things in me that they feel might be contributing to the problem and they wanted to help. I wasn't interested in that kind of help. Then. But I'm interested now." Her chin came up, and her back straightened. "Can you tell me what I need to do? I'll do whatever it takes to keep my husband and convince him our marriage is worth saving."

"Did you ask him what the trouble was?"

"I did." Her lip pulled back, almost like she hadn't been satisfied with his answer.

"And what did he say?" Kane prompted.

"He said I insult and belittle him all the time. But that's not the slightest bit true! I don't know what he meant by that, and I felt like he was just saying that so that he wouldn't tell me the real reason. At the time, I thought there was another woman. Even now... Anyone who knows my husband says that couldn't possibly be true, and there's no one who will say that he has had anything to do with anyone else, but...I don't insult and belittle him."

"Maybe you don't mean to," Kane said and didn't say anything else.

"Of course I don't mean to! I think he's incredible. He's romantic and he has great character and he's the best husband in the world. Why else would I be fighting so hard to keep him?" she said, throwing her hands up in exasperation.

"Well, if your husband is honest, then you have to believe that what he said was true."

"I'm sure he is," Selena said quickly and then said, "Wait. What do you mean? That I do insult and belittle him? But that can't..." Her voice trailed off, and although there was no dawning light in her eyes, it was obvious she was thinking.

Tiffany thought Kane would say something else, take advantage of the fact that she was wavering, but he allowed her to roll it over in her mind.

That made sense to Tiffany after she thought about it, because she didn't mind being guided in the right direction, but she resented people coming down on her like a sledgehammer, demanding she do whatever it was that they wanted her to do, without giving her the choice.

Most of the time, she would choose the reasonable decision if given time to think about it, but sometimes she would be completely unreasonable if she felt she were being pressured.

She admired Kane's wisdom.

And his patience, because it took Selena an awful long time to think.

"I guess he must be telling the truth," she eventually said, her words slow, her voice much more subdued. "But I don't know what he means." She lifted her shoulders. "I'm being honest. I truly don't know what he means."

Funny how Kane could be patient and kind, sitting on a paint bucket in the middle of an unfinished room, counseling with a woman who was having trouble with her husband, and still look rough and rugged and completely manly to her.

Tiffany had trouble keeping her eyes off of him. His mannerisms were masculine but also compassionate. It was an appealing juxtaposition of traits. Compassion mixed with masculinity. Strength mixed with kindness. Empathy mixed with uncompromising dedication to doing right.

He was a man of character. A man who would stand by his word, who would do right whether anyone else was or not. A rare and valuable man.

And he'd said he was interested in her.

But she could never counsel someone like he was doing now. She had no idea what to say to Selena. She was practically chomping at the bit to get away and would have run out of the inn if anyone else had been able to do it.

"I'll let you know a little secret," Kane finally said. He turned his head and lifted a brow at Tiffany, just a little acknowledgment of her presence, before he turned back to Selena. "Men have fragile egos. What might seem like a suggestion on your part may sound like an insult on his. So you might be suggesting that he, for example, move his toothbrush to the other side of the sink. It sounds like a perfectly reasonable suggestion to you. But he might be hearing you say, 'I don't like where you put your toothbrush, you don't do it right, and that makes you a moron.'"

Kane lifted a hand. "I know that's a silly example. But if you're constantly giving 'suggestions,'" he made air quotes with his fingers, "then that's constantly sounding like insults to him, and it could be part of your disconnect."

Kane's voice was gentle and reasonable, and Tiffany almost forgot to listen to the words, no matter how wise they were, because of the soothing cadence.

"But what should I do if he's doing something that needs to be corrected? I mean, I don't care where he puts his toothbrush, as long as he puts it in the holder and not on the sink. Because if he did, I would say something about it. Should I not say anything?" Selena asked, like it was obvious it was totally okay for her to ask her husband to move his toothbrush.

"That's really not the point. I'm telling you, men have fragile egos. In a normal marriage, asking to move his toothbrush is not a big deal. But in a marriage where he feels insulted and belittled all the time, I would be very careful with the things I asked him to do. In fact, if you're really willing to do anything, then I would stop with all of my 'suggestions.'" He did the air quotes again. "And I would only say good things to him."

Selena looked like she was digesting that, and this time, Kane went on.

"So let me ask you, if the toothbrush is on the counter, and you want him to put it in the holder. That's where it belongs. It's a perfectly reasonable request, but why don't you just pick it up and put it in the holder if that's where you want it?"

"Because I'm not his mother. It's not hard to put the toothbrush in the holder instead of on the sink."

Kane lifted both his hands, like he was innocent, because Selena's voice was getting a little irritated. "Is it worth your marriage?" he asked simply.

Her erect posture slumped, and she looked down. "No."

"You want to know what you can do to save your marriage—give up a little."

His words were spoken compassionately, but they made her jaw clench. "I'm just supposed to give up everything while he gets everything? He gets a maid, cook, washerwoman, and someone who agrees with his every word and doesn't complain?"

"I thought you said he was a good man?"

"I did." She sighed and looked away.

"Do you really think he's going to take advantage of you like that?"

"That's what you're telling me to do."

"If he agrees to give you a chance to show you've changed, then you need to show that you've actually changed. And part of that would be if you said you're willing to do whatever it takes, then *do* whatever it takes. Don't give him any suggestions, no matter how badly you think he needs them, unless he asks you. That's not for the rest of your marriage. Of course you have a voice, of course he should welcome your suggestions, but make sure you're not giving him a suggestion every time you open your mouth."

That was the strongest counsel that Kane had uttered, and Tiffany's eyes widened just slightly, expecting Selena to buck and kick. She hadn't taken any of it very well, as much as she said she was willing to do anything, but Tiffany supposed for some people it was hard to give up control.

She also was impressed that Kane seemed to know that. And he seemed to have an intuitive sense of when he could push and when he needed to back off.

He was born for this role. He excelled in it. Unlike her, with her history that would make the devil blush.

She wanted to get up and walk out. Now that she had proof right in front of her eyes that she would never be good enough.

"So you think I do this for a month or two, then I'll convince him that I'm not attacking his ego every time I ask him to do something?"

"That's possible, but if you go into this thinking 'okay, in a month or two I go back to being what I used to be,' you're going to go back to having what you have right now."

"I see. So I have to become a completely new person."

"When you accept Christ, you do become a new person. Maybe, it's just a matter of you growing into that person."

"Your counsel sounds an awful lot like the wife needs to be a doormat so the man can do whatever he wants."

"I don't think it has anything to do with men and women. Although there definitely are specific commands for wives and husbands according to the Bible. You can ignore them if you want to." Kane shrugged like it didn't make any difference to him whether she followed the Bible or not. "But there are also specific commands that are gender neutral. If you're a Christian, you're commanded to serve others and to treat them like Christ, giving up your will for his." He spread his hands out, his elbows resting on his knees. "Isn't that what this is? Giving up what you want, for someone else. It's not a matter of the wife being a doormat. It's a matter of you doing what the Bible tells you to do. Becoming a servant and serving others rather than yourself. The 'others' you're serving just happen to be your husband. The command is that we put others first, and we serve them in love, not expecting anything in return. If you do that in your marriage, I promise you, you'll have a good one. Especially if you're married to a good man."

It was almost like he wanted to add something and then didn't.

Tiffany figured there were probably men who would take advantage of a wife who was willing to serve her husband and not expect anything in return.

It took another ten minutes, but by the time Kane was finished, Selena was convinced that his way would work. Not because it was Kane's way, but because it was the way that God commanded. And since He was God, He could do those things.

Selena shook their hands, her face looking happy, and almost peaceful, for the first time.

"Thank you so much. I can't wait to go home and talk to my husband about this. I feel like my eyes have been opened for the first time even though I've been trying for months to be able to see." She smiled at Kane and then at Tiffany. "Thank you for taking the time to talk to me."

"It's my job," Kane said simply, and after another thank you, Selena rushed out.

Kane turned toward Tiffany, but she spoke first.

"You are amazing. I've never seen anyone counsel before, and that was just...astounding. You seem to know exactly what to say and when to say it. And honestly when she first came in here and started talking about being a doormat, I didn't think you were going to get through to her. But you did."

"You couldn't see, but I was praying. I don't have the right words on my own. I just pray. Pray that God will supply them, and He did. Despite me."

"What do you mean despite you? It's not despite you, it's because of you."

"No. It's because of God. It's because of what His word says, and what He brought to my mind, and how He was working in her heart."

He lifted a shoulder. "And that was the prayer. That God would work. Through me, yes, but God working."

"I didn't even think to pray. I should have been, shouldn't I?" she said thoughtfully, then a little sadly. Not only was she a failure as a counselor, she couldn't even be a success as a support.

"I wanted to thank you."

"For what?" she asked, trying not to sound annoyed. She hadn't done anything. She'd just sat there like a log. A stone could have done a better job of being support.

"For being there. Being *here*. I didn't need someone to talk or to say anything. I just needed you here."

"So anybody would do?" she said, sadness leaking into her words. She also didn't want to be just anybody. She wanted to be what he needed.

"No. I needed someone I was comfortable with. Someone who wasn't going to interrupt me when I was talking. You appreciated the times of silence I had, understood that they were necessary to let her think. You would be shocked at the number of times I've counseled people and have been interrupted by someone who wanted to add to what I was saying or, worse yet, correct me. Plus, it just meant a lot to me to have you here. Thank you."

"Hey, Kane, I'm done with the sink, but I'll leave the glue there if you want it," Dr. John said as he stuck his head in the partially open door.

Kane turned his head but didn't stand up. "Thanks, man. I'll be right there."

"Sounds good. When you're done with that tile, we can get the floor down and we might be able to finish today." Dr. John slipped back out, waving a hand at Tiffany. She waved back, but he was gone.

"I probably better go."

"Yeah. I need to go too. There's no one else working the front desk."

"All right. We're still on to watch the kids?"

If she weren't so annoyed with herself, she might think that he was asking her just because he didn't want to leave or was looking for something to say to prolong their conversation, but that couldn't be it, so she just nodded her head and said a subdued, "Yes."

"All right. Thanks again."

He gave her another look before standing and walking out.

Chapter 14

DAWN HAD NOT YET BROKEN when Kane pulled up to the children's center. There were lights on in the window, and as his headlights swiped across the lot, they flashed across Tiffany's car in front of him.

She'd beat him here.

It didn't surprise him. If she said she was going to be somewhere, she was always ten minutes early. She might not have a clue as to what she was going to do, but she was there and willing to do any job that anyone gave her.

She also took instruction well.

It was too bad he hadn't had more time to talk to her that day at the inn, because after the counseling session, she had been subdued and seemed off.

They had the room that Dr. John and he were working on already booked, and he knew he wouldn't be able to work on it over the weekend, so he'd wanted to get it finished. Otherwise, he wouldn't have left her.

Whether it was the counsel he gave or something else, he wanted to get it straightened out.

He was almost positive she wasn't angry, just seemed distant. Probably that's why he was looking forward to today so much.

He knocked on the door softly and tried the knob which was unlocked. So he pushed in.

Miss Kendall and Tiffany were standing in front of him talking softly.

Tiffany was holding something that looked a little bit like a football except...

Kane tilted his head.

Tiffany was holding a baby.

He was sure of it.

He walked cautiously forward. After all, the last time he'd been at the children's home, just a few days ago, there had been no baby. Just Haley, Sammy, Lori and Ryan. Jasmine had gone to her new home, and from what Miss Kendall reported back to them, she was mostly happy there. Another four siblings who had been at the home for a few weeks had gone back to relatives in Chicago.

He hoped it worked out for all of them.

"A baby?" he asked softly, knowing he should be talking to Miss Kendall, but he couldn't seem to make his eyes go anywhere but Tiffany.

"Isn't he sweet?" Tiffany asked, her eyes shining and looking up at him.

"I guess," he said, almost sounding choked.

"You didn't even look at him," Tiffany accused, humor dancing in her eyes but also a reserve that hadn't been there before, keeping them shuttered.

How could he look at the baby when all he wanted to do was stare at her?

He moved his eyeballs deliberately to the baby, counted to three, and then looked back at Tiffany.

"He's adorable," Kane said, clearly communicating to her that he would agree with whatever she said about the baby, since he knew nothing about babies.

Absolutely nothing.

But if she said he was adorable, or sweet, or whatever, he'd go with it.

"Okay, I'm sorry to spring this on you guys, but he was dropped off last night, and when I got the phone call, I couldn't turn him down. He's the full brother of Ryan and half sibling to Haley and Sammy. It's a mixed-up family, but they're all together under this roof." Miss Kendall's eyes shone. "If I have them all together, there is the possibility that someone might want to adopt them, and they could all go to the same family."

Her voice was pitched low, because of the three little kids who were still sleeping, not to mention the baby was... Kane wasn't sure exactly what the baby was doing. The eyes were squinted, not really closed but not really opened either.

"That would be amazing. When you don't have a stable home, at least having your siblings with you gives you some kind of foundation and grounding. A support system if you would," Tiffany said, like she knew what she was talking about.

He wanted to ask how she knew it, but not now with Miss Kendall standing there.

"Exactly. So I'm working on that now, but in the meantime, like I said, I couldn't turn him down even though I knew I was leaving today. I have all the instructions on the counter. I have a casserole made, and all you have to do is put it in the oven, and all the baby's things are in his room, except the ones that are in the baby bag right there if you should happen to need to go anywhere. Which since there are two of you, I assumed someone could just stay here. But whatever. The car seat and the baby bag are right there."

"Got it," Tiffany said, acting like she really did have it.

"All right. I'm gonna get going so I can get back. It might be late before I get home. Bedtime is on the sheet, and I usually try to stick to it pretty closely, otherwise they wake up at the same time the next morning with less sleep and they're grouchy." She smiled, but her eyes held the seriousness of someone who expected bedtime to be obeyed.

"Got it. Kids go to bed at bedtime, no exceptions," Kane said. He could handle bedtime. That would be the easy part.

Miss Kendall raised an eyebrow at him, then looked between the two of them with a little smile before walking with businesslike strides out the door.

"I can't believe that she does this by herself. I mean, this is her life," Tiffany said, her eyes on the baby as she swayed back and forth and bounced gently.

"She does a great job, but you're right. This is a big job for someone. It's like being a single mom, only with no hope of help, and knowing that someone might come in and pull the children out from underneath you at any moment. I would think that would be hard," Kane murmured, not really wanting to talk about Miss Kendall but completely fine having a conversation with Tiffany. Even if they were talking about tree bark, he'd be happy, as long as he was talking to her.

He felt like he needed to add, "But she does have help. She just doesn't have someone helping her full time. I guess it's kind of like a mother's helper."

"That makes it a little easier. And that's good for her. Because it sounds like she's constantly trying to find parents for the children that are placed here."

"I think so, although I don't think it's a priority." He took a chance and changed the subject. "You look like you've held a baby a time or two before."

"I had a roommate once that had a little one. He would sleep all day and cry all night. Sometimes I would stay up with him so she could sleep. I couldn't get him to stop crying, but I guess it made us both feel better if someone was holding him while he cried rather than allowing him to cry by himself."

"Did she take him to the doctor's to see why he was crying so much?" he asked, unsure if that was normal.

"The doctor said he just had days and nights mixed up, and there was nothing to do but try to get him to sleep less during the day and more at night."

"It seems like it would be hard to reason with a baby like that."

"Yeah. That's what we thought when she came home and told me what he said. But I guess he expected us to wake up the sleeping baby during the day, banking on the fact that it would help him sleep at night."

"That worked?"

"Actually, it didn't. He was just up more during the day and still cried at night. I think he did that for about four weeks, which felt like six years."

"I haven't been around too many babies, but a baby's cry can make you feel like running."

"I guess that's the way God designed it so that someone would come and do something about them."

"I can't figure out if he's awake or asleep. Do you know?" He leaned a little closer, and originally he was thinking about the baby, but he caught a whiff of Tiffany's scent, which made him lean closer. Some kind of subtle flowery scent with just enough sweetness in it to make him breathe deeply.

He'd smelled it often when working with her in the church, but this was the first time that he'd really been close enough and paying attention to think about it. It was a scent that suited her and one that he associated with smiles and laughter and sweet support.

"He's awake. Don't you see his eyes blinking every once in a while?"

"He doesn't have his eyes open very far."

"Some babies don't. Although some babies' eyes are wide open—my roommate's was. From the time she brought him home from the hospital, he looked around at everything. Such a sweetheart. I've lost touch with her." Her voice trailed off, almost as though she didn't really want to talk anymore about her roommate and just realized that she shouldn't have been doing it in the first place.

"So how old would the baby be now?"

"Elementary school age, I think. Maybe junior high. I'd have to sit down and think about it. Goodness, life goes by fast."

"Tell me about it."

She started walking over to the couch. "I'm going to sit down for a bit. I think as long as he's happy, I'm going to hold him. Miss Kendall said the other kids wouldn't be up for at least an hour."

"That's still really early. Did she say they usually get up that early?"

"They do. And she said they get up at that time no matter what time she puts them to bed, so that's why she is so strict about bedtime."

"I see. Did she say what time bedtime was?" he asked, wondering how much time he'd have to spend with Tiffany by himself, once the kids went to bed.

"Eight o'clock on the dot."

"That's not bad. We can handle it," he said, his voice maybe lacking the conviction it might have had if he'd been talking about handling something that he was comfortable with, say, sermon notes or drywall.

Babies, not so much.

"I got the feeling that you weren't very happy when we were done talking to Selena. I was wondering if you'd tell me what the problem was?" There didn't seem to be a reason to beat around the bush or not say the things that needed to be said. Maybe he should be more subtle, but he wanted to be able to talk to Tiffany honestly, without pulling punches.

If that's what he wanted, it's probably what he should try to do.

One hand came up, and she touched the baby's soft cheek, smiling at him as he nuzzled his head toward her finger.

Maybe she wasn't going to answer him. He had been pretty bold in asking.

"I just felt like a failure. You know? I don't know how to counsel. I had no clue what to say to that woman. None. And I realized I should have been praying for you. But I just sat there. It made me realize that...that I wasn't good at it."

"It was your first time. And you weren't counseling, you were just there. Just as a third person so that I wasn't closed up in a room with a woman by myself. Because once a thing like that happens, it's her word against mine, and sometimes... I know it's hard to believe that sometimes people get upset with the pastor, but that's a really good way to get him fired. Even just the accusation, with no facts to back it up, can make a man lose his job."

"Really? Someone can lie about you and you lose your job?"

"I know men it's happened to. I don't want to be one of them."

Like she found it hard to believe, she shook her head. But then she said, "I was glad to be there."

"Sometimes, that's all it takes. But you have a natural empathy, so don't sell yourself short. Also, you're great with kids." He nodded at the baby. "You never had any?"

"No."

He wanted to push. Wanted to talk more about moving forward, but he figured he didn't want to scare her. Still, rather than just assume she wasn't interested, there would be no harm in asking.

"When Miss Kendall walked in on us the other day, I told you I was interested. You never really replied, and I thought maybe that was the problem. I don't want to make things awkward today, because we're going to be working together with the children, but I just wondered if maybe I'm pushing too hard, and you don't really like me."

There. He hadn't laid out his whole hand, but he'd given her the opportunity to tell him no.

"I like you, Kane."

He couldn't help it. His heart trembled at her use of his name. Such an odd reaction, but typical of his reactions to her.

"But?" he made himself say.

"But I'm not right for you. You need someone who can be what you need them to be. Not like me. Not with my background."

"And that is?"

"First of all, I went to church when I was a kid, but I never paid attention. I blew it off as much as I could and honestly only went because I was forced or because my friends were there. That's for starters."

"God doesn't give you background checks when He calls you to His work." It wasn't what he wanted to say, not really, but it was applicable.

"I know."

"He's interested in your heart right now, and if you're willing to work, He's willing to use you."

"I know, and I can be used in the church, but it's a little different to be with you."

"And how is that?"

"You know."

He didn't want to get into that, it would just be a dead-end argument, so instead he tried to grasp on the positive thing she had said. "You like me?"

Chapter 15

TIFFANY LOOKED SO SWEET, so maternal, sitting there holding the baby, looking at Kane under her lashes, giving him a look that said, *do I really have to repeat this?*

Then her eyes dropped, and she nodded.

"You don't really seem like a shy, retiring type." He teased her just a little.

Like he thought, her eyes flashed. "I'm not. I just...there's no point in me admitting that I like you when there's no future for us."

"When the church hired me, I didn't tell them what I had done before I became a pastor. They didn't ask."

"Really? What about references?"

"Oh, I had to give references. I did tell them where I got my degree, who I'd served under, but as for previous jobs, they didn't ask."

"Okay. So does that matter?"

"I kind of feel like I have to tell you what I used to be, since you seem to think our pasts are so important, but also because I wouldn't want someone who decides to be with me to be blindsided by my past when it shows up at our door. Somehow, your past always finds you, doesn't it?"

It was a true statement, because yeah, your past was always there just waiting to find you out.

"I guess. Actually, yes. That's part of my problem."

He really wanted to know what it was that scared her about what she used to do. How bad could it be?

It couldn't be as bad as his.

"Well, can I ask you to tell me again that you might like me, before I tell you something that might make you hate me forever?"

"Seriously? You're not going to tell me anything that you used to do that's going to change the way I look at you now."

"Oh, I bet I can."

"No. You have character. And I meant what I said about your ability to counsel. I've sat under your sermons, and they're not too long, so that makes them good."

"I'm not laughing." His laugh belied his words.

"I was kidding. Seriously, you have a knack for being able to say everything that needs to be said, and not too much, losing your audience. I always leave challenged but not discouraged. That's not an easy thing. And I admire it."

"Thanks. That's one of the nicest things anyone could have said to me." He had to admit he was surprised. He hadn't been fishing for compliments and hadn't expected her to say something that he admitted was one of his goals. To touch people like that.

"It's true."

"Is that you saying you like me?" He was pushing, but he needed her to admit it again, if she could.

"I do. I like you a lot. More than I've ever liked anyone else before. If you must know, most of the time, when I was after a man, or interested in him, it was because of his pocketbook."

He admired her for being able to admit it, but still, he was going to shock her.

"I don't know what kind of life you led before, so you may not know what I'm talking about, but there's a whole party scene in big cities, male escorts, strip clubs, you can hire a man for your bachelorette party. Get them to jump out of a cake if you'd like. You know?"

He'd been watching her face, and her eyes had widened, almost like panic, and then she ducked her head, her fingers coming up and touching the blanket on the baby, her head studiously lowered so that he couldn't even see her lashes.

"I used to do that."

Her head jerked up, eyes open wide, mouth opened almost as far.

"You were a stripper?" she asked, disbelief in her tone.

"I was." He smiled, although he knew it wasn't a good smile. It was an I'm forcing myself to smile, but there's nothing funny, and I don't really feel like it smile.

He pointed to his face, making circles around it. "You see this?"

"I do. You're handsome." Then she nodded. "You must have been a weightlifter as well."

He nodded. Surprised, then thoughtful over her words.

"Where's Miss Kendall?" a little voice said beside them.

He tried not to look disappointed or, even worse, frustrated as he turned his head to look at the little one who had walked into the room, blanket trailing behind her.

"Sammy, good morning," Tiffany said, giving him time to get his feelings under control. Eight o'clock tonight seemed like an awful long time to wait, but if that's what he needed to do, he would.

"Good morning," Sammy said, one fist rubbing her eyes. "Where's Miss Kendall?"

"She had to go home today. She's gonna come back late tonight. Do you remember that you have a day off school today?" Tiffany said, sounding excited and smiling at Sammy.

"Hmmm. I forgot she told me you guys were coming." She took the blanket and wrapped it around her shoulders, walking the rest of the way to the couch and climbing up. "Miss Kendall said you'd be keeping all of us and Isaac too. And that Pastor Kane was going to help you."

"That's right. She gave me a whole list of instructions, which I might need help reading. Do you think you can help me?"

"As long as the words aren't too big. Big words are hard. But I can read little words."

"I think most of these words are little."

"And I can't read cursive yet. So if it's in cursive, you'll have to read it."

"I can do that, if it's in cursive. And you can read it if it's not."

Sammy smiled, snuggled closer. "Can I hold the baby?"

Tiffany's lips pulled up, and her eyes met Kane's.

She didn't seem to be upset with him, didn't seem to be overly shocked or annoyed or disgusted. Maybe his past wouldn't bother her.

He stood up. "I'm going over here and reading these mysterious instructions. Or maybe I'll just bring them back over for you to read for me, Sammy."

"I'm holding the baby. You have to read them yourself," Sammy said, very matter-of-factly, as she held her arms out and Tiffany put the baby in them, careful to support the head and keep her hand underneath the crook of her arm.

The morning went fairly quickly, with Kane making breakfast while Tiffany talked to Sammy and supervised the holding of the baby. Eventually Haley got up, and then she was thrown into the mix of holding the baby until breakfast was ready. Ryan was last to get up just as the scrambled eggs and toast were ready. The kids seemed happy with it, and Tiffany seemed if not impressed, at least pleased that he was able to cook.

He could as long as it wasn't anything fancy, but he supposed he didn't need fancy, he just needed to be fed. That had always been his motto anyway.

By lunchtime, he was ready for a nap, and the kids were, too. At least little Isaac had fussed only twice, both times because he was hungry.

And then, when he went down for a nap, the kids begged to play a game, so he looked at Tiffany. "Blindman's bluff?"

"Oh, I'm playing too?" she asked, grinning.

"Yay," Haley and Sammy said, not hearing the question in her voice and apparently assuming she was going to play. They jumped up and down beside her.

"That good with you?" he asked Ryan, who was a little more sedate but still looked eager.

"I don't think I've played that before. Is it fun?"

Haley and Sammy quit jumping up and down and looked to him.

"Is it fun?" Sammy asked, as if the question had just occurred to her when Ryan gave it voice.

Three pairs of expectant eyes looked at him.

"Of course. I wouldn't have suggested it if it weren't. But we do need something long that we can tie around your face."

It took a little bit, but they finally found a T-shirt that could be folded up longways and that fit around everyone's faces.

He explained the rules to them, keeping it down to a bare minimum, giving specific boundaries, and telling the kids they had to stay in their hiding spot until the blindfolded person found them.

The few times he'd played growing up, they'd always ended up running around, but in his experience, the blindfolded person could get hurt, because they would get excited and start running and forget they couldn't see and run into something.

Each kid had had a turn being blindfolded, and he'd gotten one as well, when Sammy tagged Tiffany, and it was her turn to be it.

"What if I'm afraid of the dark?" she said as he took the blindfold from Sammy's face and walked toward her.

"It's not dark out. Look." He pointed at the window, where the sun shone in.

"But it'll be dark under the blindfold," Tiffany said, which made Sammy giggle.

"Are you really afraid of the dark?" Ryan asked.

"No, but I figured it couldn't hurt to ask."

"She's just trying to get out of her turn," Kane said, reaching her, taking her shoulders, and spinning her around.

As he tied the blindfold, the kids found their hiding places, with Sammy imitating what Kane had done several times, which was sit in the middle of the floor. Typically, people thought the best hiding places were behind a chair or another piece of furniture, but he'd found when he'd played with his friends as a kid that those were the first places people looked, but it was hard to look at an entire floor when one was blindfolded.

It hadn't taken long for the kids to catch on, and it was one of the more successful and popular spots.

Keeping a hold of Tiffany's shoulders, he spun her around three times.

"All right, can you see?" he asked.

"I have my eyes closed."

"I don't think she answered the question, did she?" he said, lifting a brow at the children.

"You didn't answer the question!" Ryan said from his spot over by the armchair.

"Ryan's that way," Tiffany said, pointing her hand toward the direction the voice had come.

Ryan snapped his mouth closed, his eyes wide, like he'd been tricked into talking and now she knew where he was hiding.

Kane laughed as he stepped away from Tiffany. "All right, give me about five seconds to hide, and then you can start looking. Be careful, don't break a toe or anything," he said, winking at Sammy on the floor so close to Tiffany that if Tiffany sat down, she could lean over and touch her.

"Thanks. Your concern for my toes is endearing."

"Good to hear. I'm glad you noticed."

He walked over, just beyond Sammy, and sat down on the middle of the couch, pulling his feet up so that his entire body was on the couch. If she patted over the periphery, she might miss him.

He hadn't really considered that he was directly in the line of where she would fall if she tripped over Sammy. Which was what happened five seconds later.

Chapter 16

TIFFANY WAS LOOKING forward to eight o'clock but dreading it as well. She wasn't sure whether Kane had actually been serious, but it was like he'd asked Selena when he was counseling. Is your husband an honest man? Would he lie about it?

She could answer those questions. Kane was an honest man. He wouldn't lie. So he wouldn't have been teasing her about whether or not he had been a stripper before he became a preacher.

It boggled her mind. But it also made her feel like...maybe there was a chance for them.

Except, he hadn't said he'd been married before.

He might not be interested in being someone's fourth husband.

Not to mention she might not be interested in saying vows a fourth time.

It seemed like there was no point. They hadn't made a difference the first three times—she hadn't kept them. It seemed almost sacrilege to keep making vows she kept not keeping.

She wasn't always very good at putting things out of her mind—normally they sat in there and she chewed on them—but she didn't usually get to watch kids, and she considered it a treat. After all, she would probably never have children of her own, and if she only got to spend a couple of days a month with them, she wanted to enjoy it.

Not to mention, she'd never played blindman's bluff before. She found it fun and a little exciting, but that was all about Kane playing with her and less about her actually loving the game.

Just something about playing with him livened things up and kept her on her toes. Made it fun.

This was her first time being blindfolded, and she had to admit maybe she started out a little bit too fast. Because she only took two steps and tripped over something she hadn't noticed on the floor before.

Of course, she'd seen the kids hiding on the floor, but catching them on the floor pretty much meant she had to get down on her hands and knees and swipe her arms around, because if she was walking, it was pretty much a given that she was going to miss them. Unless she made a beeline to them on accident, which is what she did.

She barely had time to let out a startled "oh!" before she went flailing forward.

Vaguely, she remembered the couch was there somewhere and hoped she hit it in such a way that she didn't knock her head.

That was the last coherent thought she had before she went flailing forward and landed in a hard lap. Strong arms came around her and cushioned her fall.

She had to laugh. "I think I found someone."

"Is that what you're doing? Finding people? Because I feel attacked." Kane's voice rumbled in her ear, and her grin widened.

"Women just throw themselves at you, don't they?" There was definitely flirt in her voice. Why not? He said he liked her, and she liked him. Why not flirt?

"Maybe they do, but I don't typically catch them. I guess that makes you special."

There was flirt in his voice too. She liked it for sure.

"My goodness. Special." Maybe she would have said more, but he pulled her blindfold off, and she hadn't realized how close she was to his face.

"That's right. Special." His voice was lower and softer, meant for her ears only. It sounded like an endearment.

"I'll take it," she said.

"I was having fun with the kids, but I kind of wish it were bedtime, and we just put them down."

"Pastor Kane is 'it!'" Ryan shouted, running across the room and jumping on top of them.

Kane grunted, and maybe she did too a little, but she slipped to one side and wedged herself between the couch and his body.

Of course, the girls wouldn't let Ryan jump on the pastor without them, and they landed on them in short order until they were all squished on the couch, laughing and bouncing.

"Not sure how I got on the bottom of this pile," Kane said, his eyes twinkling, "but I'm pretty sure I got the short end of the stick. I might say that, except...I think I like it."

She had to smile, and maybe she wished the kids were in bed too, but they weren't, so she said, "I wonder if Pastor Kane is ticklish?"

"He's not," Kane said quickly. Too quickly.

She laughed, her wicked evil laugh. "Let's find out, guys!" And she ran her fingers over his ribs, wiggling them.

It turned out Kane was very ticklish but not so ticklish that he didn't have enough strength left to roll, turning and dumping them all off the couch and onto the floor where he landed on top of them, careful not to squish anyone, moving his own fingers around, tickling them back.

All they needed was a dog running around barking and licking their faces to make it a family scene out of a good movie.

The thought sobered her.

She'd never thought she'd be part of a family in any kind of a movie.

But she found that there was a certain amount of security and fun comfortableness as they played together.

Why couldn't she be part of a family?

Didn't Kane tell Selena that it was up to her to do the changing?

Hadn't Tiffany decided she was going to change?

If she wanted a family, why not go for it?

Chapter 17

"I TRIED TO KNOCK, BUT no one answered the door," a voice above them said, startling Tiffany, and she rolled over, looking over her shoulder at the elegant woman who was standing on the other side of the couch, purse over her shoulder, stylish hat set at an angle over her head, and a fitted jacket that looked like it had been made for style and not warmth.

"I'm sorry? You knocked?" Tiffany said, struggling to get up and away from the little hands that wanted to keep tickling her.

"I don't mean to interrupt you. I can come back," the woman said, looking a little tragic, like there was a deep sadness and sorrow in her life, and she'd never quite been able to overcome it.

"No? Truly. Please stay." Tiffany felt a little off balance, since she was struggling to get to her knees before climbing awkwardly to her feet, with one kid hanging on her arm and Kane's legs getting tangled up with hers.

He apparently hadn't seen the newcomer yet, or she assumed he would be trying to get into a slightly more pastor-worthy position.

"Please forgive us. I guess we're just big kids, but we don't get to watch children very often, and we're having a pretty good time pretending we're still children ourselves, I guess," Tiffany said, rambling a little and struggling to remember a time in her life when she'd felt any more at a disadvantage. This woman was elegance refined, and Tiffany was most definitely not.

"It thrills my heart to see you all having such a great time," the lady said, her voice cultured.

She held out a perfectly manicured hand, and Tiffany wiped her hand, sticky from feeding the kids apples just before they decided to play blindman's bluff, on her leg and resisted the urge to spit on it and rub it again.

She grabbed the other lady's hand. "I'm Tiffany."

"I'm Beverly."

Kane finally realized someone was there, apparently, since the noise abruptly ceased, and behind her, all movement stopped until Kane struggled to get to his knees and then his feet.

"Miss Beverly," he said, his words calm despite the struggle he'd just gone through to stand.

"Pastor Kane. I don't think we've ever met each other under quite these circumstances," the lady said.

"Nope. You're absolutely right. Usually I'm a little more dignified, but today's kid day." He lifted a shoulder. And while he had been eager to stand, he didn't seem overly needful to impress anyone.

Tiffany appreciated that about him, that, despite this lady's obvious elegance, which just screamed she had money, and Tiffany would know, because she'd run in those circles for years, Kane was simply himself and not trying to impress anyone.

He also wiped his hand on his pant leg before he shook Beverly's proffered hand.

"Is there anything I can do for you?" Tiffany asked.

"Normally I stop in once a month or so, just to meet with Miss Kendall and make sure things are going okay. Make sure she has everything she needs and that the contribution I'm making to keep this open is sufficient and doesn't need to be increased."

"Oh, I'm sorry. Miss Kendall isn't here. She went home to see friends and get some Christmas shopping done."

"Normally, I let her know, but I was in town and wanted to stop here first. This is one of my favorite places."

Just then the baby started crying, and Tiffany gave an apologetic shrug. "I'm sorry. I need to go get him."

"Do you mind if I come too?"

"Not at all," she said, giving Kane a glance over her shoulder. He'd read the situation perfectly and was gathering up the kids, telling them that they could go into the other room where the bookshelf was and pick out some books to read for a bit.

If the kids were upset that they were done playing blindman's bluff and having tickling contests, they didn't look like it as they cheered and ran toward the doorway.

"So much life and energy and happiness," Beverly said, shaking her head.

"It's hard not to be in a good mood whenever the kids are smiling at you and begging you to play with them. In fact, you can't play with them and stay in a bad mood."

It's not that Tiffany had been in such a bad mood, although she had been shocked with Kane's declaration, but she'd been slowly starting to get used to it and realizing that everything that applied to her applied to him as well. That might be what he used to be, but it wasn't what he was now.

She'd been around him enough to see his character, the grace and love he showed, the kindness and compassion. The empathy. The wisdom. The obvious dedication to trying to live a holy and blameless life.

Those weren't things that grew overnight, and obviously, they couldn't grow if he were still living a life of sin.

Also, it just made sense that if he were still living that life, he wouldn't confess it.

By the time they reached the edge of the crib, little Isaac had gone into full-throated baby screams that only diminished a little as Tiffany picked him up.

"I think he'll need his diaper changed, and then he'll need to be fed." She felt a little uncertain as she looked at Beverly taking off her jacket.

On impulse, she said, "Would you like to hold him?"

"Could I?" Beverly said, as though the thought hadn't occurred to her.

"Of course. You can change his diaper too, if you'd like to. I can get the bottle ready."

"Oh... I'm not sure. I've never changed a diaper."

"You never had children?" Tiffany never had either, and it was a source of sadness for her. Although she hadn't longed for children like some women she'd heard of, she'd always thought they would be in her future someday.

Today, she'd felt that longing. That desire for family anyway.

"I did," Beverly said, surprising her yet again.

"I didn't know." Not that she heard that much about Beverly around town. Other than she was a benefactor and a lot of the reason for Blueberry Beach's prosperity.

"Not many people know or maybe even remember. I was young." She lifted a brow and gave Tiffany a look as though wondering whether or not she should admit how young. "Fifteen," she said, and Tiffany bit back her gasp of surprise.

"She was born healthy, a beautiful baby, but she died in the night. Back then, and maybe even now, they just didn't know, couldn't explain. I couldn't afford an autopsy, and the insurance wouldn't cover it. Maybe it wouldn't have been conclusive either. Sometimes, these things just happen."

Tiffany stood still, not knowing what to do, because the memory was obviously painful for Beverly.

"I'm so sorry. That's a loss you regret and a constant source of sadness," she said, thinking about how she'd feel if she'd lost a baby.

"I'm sad, I can't deny it. But to say it was a bad thing, I just can't. After all, I went on to be quite successful in the business world, and I wouldn't have been if my baby had lived. I was planning on keeping her, and it would have been very difficult for me to have done anything aside from some kind of low-wage, no-outlet job. Not that money buys happiness, because I don't think it does." She sighed. "But God obviously had a plan for my life, and everything worked out. I can say that because I know I'll see the baby in heaven someday."

"That's something to look forward to."

She didn't have any babies in heaven or anywhere, and she hadn't felt the lack more acutely than she had today.

Isaac started fussing again, breaking the sad atmosphere that had settled between them.

"I'll go get a bottle made, if you think you're gonna be okay."

"I think so." Beverly looked around, holding the baby who had quieted somewhat in her arms, bouncing him gently as she walked over and grabbed a diaper from the pile before setting him down on the changing table, her face holding the look that a woman often gets when she's looking at a baby.

It was beautiful to watch, but Isaac would be wanting his bottle and demanding it quite loudly, so Tiffany hurried out.

Kane stood at the counter, filling up cups of water when she walked into the kitchen.

"You lost the children?" she asked.

He startled, like he hadn't heard her coming, and he gave her a once-over. "And you lost the baby. I guess we'll both get fired."

"That doesn't say much of anything good about us, does it? Our first day on the job, and we can't even keep track of our charges."

"Hey, I'm a pastor, not a babysitter."

"And I own one third of an inn, which is my sole claim to fame."

"You didn't exist in a vacuum up until the day you moved back to Blueberry Beach," he said, his eyes studying her.

"No, you're right. I guess everyone has skeletons in their closet, and I suppose, if nothing else crazy happens, when the children go to bed, I will crack my closet door and give you a peek."

"I'm not too big on skeletons, but I do want to know what's in your closet at least, so I'm going to take you up on that," he said, setting the cup down and walking closer to her as she stood with the bottle in her hand.

"Look at that. We've got so much in common, because I'm not too much for skeletons either."

"So we're counting the things we have in common?"

"Isn't that why people get together? Because they have things in common?"

"I suppose. Or maybe it's just because they see someone they think the Lord might have put in their path for that specific reason."

She wanted to roll her eyes and laugh. He thought God put her in his path and God wanted him to be with her? Improbable. Not just improbable, impossible.

It was so tempting to tell him so too, but she just couldn't. She couldn't laugh at that, because he seemed so serious and like he truly believed it.

She admired him and respected him and believed in him enough that if he believed in it, she wasn't going to scoff without a good reason.

Even if she felt like she had a good reason, because she was hardly the kind of person that God would give to a man like Kane.

"My words upset you. You don't believe they can be true."

"Was it that obvious? I was really trying to hide it."

"You need to work on that, because yeah. I pretty much read your face like a book." A thump came from the other room, and he grimaced. "Speaking of reading books, the kids are expecting me, and I told them I'd be right back with drinks. But... It's funny how hard it is for me to pull myself away from you."

"That's just attraction. Nothing substantial."

"You can be attracted to people without admiring them. You can be attracted to someone who lacks character. To someone and know that the idea is ridiculous, and you're being stupid."

"All right. I have to give you that. You're right."

"Thank you. I appreciate that."

"Go on. Go read to the kids while I make this bottle. We'll talk later."

"Go out on a date with me. Please?" he said, the words tumbling out of his mouth, like he couldn't stop them. And he hadn't made any move to go, anyway.

She loved that. Loved that he looked a little insecure, and hopeful, and eager all at once.

"Can it be something where it's just you and me and we have time to talk? Where we won't be interrupted or have a lot of people around?" she said.

It seemed like every time they tried to talk, people were interrupting them, barging in, or they got pulled in one direction or another, and if they were going to discuss anything important, it would probably be a good idea to get it done. If there wasn't going to be a second date, they'd know it.

"Sure. Anything. Whatever you want."

"That's what I want. Just you. Nothing fancy, nothing crazy."

"I can do that. It's probably a good thing." And he grinned.

She thought about a pastor's salary in a small town. It wouldn't be much, and for the first time, she wondered about that. She'd had three husbands, and they'd all been rich. Deliberately on her part.

What would it be like to be married to someone who wasn't?

It would be real.

He hadn't said anything about marriage though, and she hadn't made any decisions about whether or not she wanted to be hitching up with husband number four.

He touched her arm before he gathered the cups from the counter and carried them into the room.

She finished filling the bottle and walked into the baby's room to find Beverly just finishing changing Isaac's diaper. There was a wet spot down the front of her shirt and some type of liquid dripping from her chin.

"He got me," Beverly said before Tiffany could figure out what in the world had happened.

She still wasn't quite sure.

"Isaac?"

"Yeah. I took the diaper off, and it was like a waterfall erupting." She laughed, which stunned Tiffany almost as much as the fact that a baby could have done all of that to her. There was so much wetness down the front of her shirt.

"You mean, it squirted up in the air?"

Beverly nodded. "I didn't know it could do that either."

"Wow." She had had no idea. But her lips trembled, and she tried to bite back her smile. It was funny.

"Go ahead. You can laugh. I'm laughing, even if I'm a little bit grossed out, because my chin feels wet, and there is no doubt of what it is."

"Here, let me finish dressing him, and you can go find a shirt and a bathroom and disinfectant and whatever else it takes to clean that up," she said uncertainly. She had no idea what one did when that happened.

But she would be keeping it in mind for sure if she changed Isaac's diaper again. She would most definitely be watching out for that. Although, what exactly she was going to do to keep it from happening to her, she wasn't quite sure.

It might be a good thing to look up on the Internet.

Chapter 18

BEVERLY ENDED UP STAYING through supper and until bed-time. At that point in time, it sounded like Tiffany and Beverly were lifelong friends, with all the laughing and talking they were doing.

Not that Kane felt left out exactly, because he loved watching Tiffany be happy, and he felt like maybe she didn't have a lot of good friends, true friends, in her life before.

Plus, there weren't too many sounds in the world he'd rather hear than Tiffany laughing. He also had the feeling she hadn't done a lot of that.

Still, he couldn't say he was unhappy when Beverly left, and the children were in bed, and the baby was maybe not sleeping exactly but at least not crying.

"Man, what a great day," Tiffany said as she closed the door behind Beverly and turned around, leaning against it.

"You look exhausted," he said, just in case she didn't feel that way.

"I'm sure I must. But hopefully I look happy too?"

"You do. Beautiful and happy."

"That wasn't an invitation to lie, that was just an invitation to tell me that I don't just look tired."

"Everyone is tempted to lie at times. You know, when you really don't want to tell someone something, and your mind automatically starts trying to make up a story, and you have to stop it and make your mouth say what it's supposed to."

"You're a preacher, and you have that problem?"

"I'm a preacher, right, but I'm also a man. A human. The son of Adam. I'm not perfect. Not even close." He said that last bit, a little bit disgusted, because he got that a lot. People expected him to be perfect, and he just wasn't. Never would be, as hard as he might try.

"You know I've never had any bad experiences with preachers, but I've been around people who have, and more than anything else, I think that puts people off of church, you know?"

"Yeah. I agree. People don't want to make the change in their own lives to actually become a Christian, because they know that means giving up a lot of the sinful things they think they can't live without. But once they're in church, have decided to make that change, it's almost always the hypocrisy of someone, and most likely the pastor, that drives them to back out. I don't know that I understand though, because God knows that a pastor can't be perfect. No one can. There's bound to be hypocrisy, in the pastor and the people, and I haven't figured out how to be real, to show being real, but not be so real that people don't respect you and your position. You know what I'm saying?"

Her eyes narrowed, and she nodded thoughtfully, and he thought maybe she really did understand.

Maybe he should explain it to more people, maybe they'd understand. He just kind of figured no one would get it. It was one of those things a person couldn't understand until they lived it themselves.

"Would you like a glass of water or some of your fruit from supper?" he asked, unsure of what to say. He wanted to talk to her, wanted to know everything.

Wanted her to know there was nothing better than spending the day with her, that today had cemented in his mind that she really could be the one God had for him.

It'd been a great day, and he'd enjoyed every second. He wanted more days just like this one.

"No, thank you. But you go ahead," she said.

"I think I'll eat another sandwich. I was so busy cleaning up the spilled water, and picking up the grapes that Ryan had dropped, that I totally forgot I was still hungry."

She laughed and they walked to the kitchen together, her going to the sink and getting a glass and filling it up for him and him making a sandwich.

She sat down at the bar, and he stood on the other side, smashing his sandwich together and saying, "Thanks for a really great time today. I had fun."

"Me too. I have a feeling it would have been a lot harder if it had just been me by myself, and it makes me admire Miss Kendall."

"I agree."

"I think Miss Kendall would be perfect for you."

"Maybe she would. But she's not the one I want." He took a bite of his sandwich and chewed, swallowing before he said, "I guess I'll say it to you plainly, I want you."

"I was a call girl."

Five words, and they shocked him. Despite the fact that he had given her a shock earlier, he couldn't keep the surprise off his face.

Never let it be said that he made a mock at sin, but he had to smile.

"You're kidding."

"I'm not. I went into college determined to tell every man who asked me out yes. That developed into being pretty good at dates, which, when you are passably pretty, with a decent figure, and you're good at going out on dates, and I guess other things, that's a job where a girl can make a lot of money in a short amount of time. My family had tons of money, but I was captivated by the idea of making my own, so I did that."

"And?" he asked.

"I ended up dropping out."

"Probably figured you were making great money and what would you need a college education for, right?"

"Nailed it."

He continued to eat his sandwich, even though his appetite was mostly gone. She was obviously remorseful about what she had done, as was he. And he found it more than a little ironic that the woman the Lord had put in front of him was a woman with the exact same background as his. But maybe that's what he needed, because it was on the tip of his tongue to say she didn't need to hide it.

Except.

He had.

Who was he to say what she should do, when he was not taking his own advice?

"That's how I found my first husband. He was a regular client, and I knew he had a lot of money. He asked me to marry him, and I said yes easily. I wanted a big ring, big wedding, everything. And I got it. Except, our marriage was miserable. He lost interest rather quickly, cheated on me, and we got divorced."

"I see."

"Yeah. But I didn't, because it happened twice more. Except the last time, I got taken on the divorce settlement, and I ended up with nothing. It stunk, to say the least."

"I'm sure," he murmured, his heart hurting for her. She hadn't been lying when she said she had a past that she was ashamed of. He didn't blame her at all for not wanting to talk about it.

It didn't change how he felt about her, although it did change a little how he looked at her. Maybe with more empathy, since she'd been through more than he had dreamed. Had more guilt. No wonder she was working so hard to try to make up for it.

"Now you see why I keep saying I wouldn't make a good pastor's wife. That you need someone else," she said, her eyes downcast.

"I guess by that reasoning, I would make a terrible pastor."

"But you know so much! Maybe you have that past, but that's not you anymore."

He looked at her, wondering if she would realize what she'd said, and apply it to herself.

It took a few minutes before dawning realization spread over her face.

He smiled at her, and she shook her head.

"Yes. It can be you too," he said. Emphasizing his words.

"Why do you see more in me than what there is?" she asked, not sad, exactly, just... almost astounded that someone would look at her and see beyond her past.

"The potential to be more is in all of us. I don't know why we as humans have so much trouble seeing that. We look at someone, and we judge them for what they've done. Which is right. It's natural. You are a compilation of your past, of course. But...it's just a true blessing when someone can look at you and see, not the things that you've already done, the bad things, the mistakes, but look at you and see the potential for more. That's the way God sees each of us. He knows that we were created in His image, and could be so much more than what we ever thought we could."

"Your words are inspiring. They almost make me feel like...like I could possibly live up to what you think of me," she said, laughing a little like the idea was preposterous.

"Maybe that's why God brings people together. You know? They make each other better. They complement each other. They see things in each other that no one else sees."

"Love is blind?" Her brows were raised, her voice held irony. After all, how many times had love been blind, then the blinders fall off after the wedding?

"Maybe. Maybe we just have to work at keeping those blinders on there. Because that's what marriage is. Seeing the best in your partner and bringing that out. Doing whatever it takes to help them make them better."

"I see how you would do that with someone, but...me? I don't know how to even begin thinking about finding the best in someone and focusing on that."

Her eyes dropped, and she ran a hand along the counter before shifting and moving away from him slightly.

"I guess that's the other thing I didn't tell you."

"What's that?" For some reason, her actions made his stomach clench and his heart shimmy just a little.

"I just signed the divorce papers on my third divorce a few months ago." She swallowed, before looking up at him, meeting his eyes squarely.

She wasn't joking.

"And?" he asked, wanting to make sure that was all he was dealing with before he responded. Although he didn't really know what he was going to say. What did a man say to that?

"My track record isn't exactly great. When things get hard, I get divorced." Maybe she was striving for levity, but the shrug of her shoulders didn't convey the careless attitude she seemed to have intended. Instead, he felt a great sadness radiating off of her.

The baby started crying, and she moved to take care of him, but he stopped her with a hand on her arm.

"You've made a lot of changes. You determined in your heart that you were going to become a different person, that Christ changed you."

"That's true."

"Did he?"

"Do you really want to take that chance?"

"Marriage is always a risk. You could say that someone who's never been married before, they don't have a track record, you don't know whether they're going to stay or not."

She hadn't thought of anything like that, from the expression on her face, and he smiled a little.

"You can say that about me, since I've never been married. You have no clue what kind of husband I'm going to be, or whether I'm going to stick around, or whether I'm going to get divorced at the drop of a hat."

"I can tell that you're not going to," she said dismissively, like it was a well-known fact.

"I can tell the same about you," he said just as dismissively, imitating her tone.

"I need to get the baby."

He wasn't sure what time Miss Kendall would be getting back, and he wanted to make sure they were on the same page, so he said, "We're still on for Friday evening? I'll pick you up?"

"Yeah," she said, not sounding super excited. "I'll have to make sure I can find someone to cover for me."

"If you can't, I will. Find someone that is," he added hastily, not wanting her to think that he was going to cover for her. Obviously.

He wasn't usually so tongue-tied, but she brought out everything - all the emotions he usually kept contained. His hopes, his dreams, and maybe he was pursuing her a little too hard, pushing her too much, but he wanted her to see that she was more than what she thought she was. She was capable of anything.

He murmured softly, as his hand dropped from her arm, "I can do all things through Christ which strengtheneth me."

Her head jerked up, eyes wide, before her lips curved up just a little.

"You don't play fair," she finally said.

"There is no 'fair' to life."

"It's all about winning?"

"Not at all. It's about doing God's will and bringing glory to Him."

"And somehow you would do that being with me?"

"There's not a doubt in my mind - not one - that I am meant to be with you." It was true. Everything had fallen into place tonight. Seeing her with the baby, playing Blind Man's Bluff with her, the talk that they'd had, and realizing that her past was just the same as his. He had those doubts and the guilt and other things that had plagued him from time to time, despite knowing that Christ had forgiven everything.

Seeing it from outside himself, looking at her, seeing how simple it was for her to be forgiven, and to work out of love, and not out of duty.

God had used Tiffany to show him what he needed himself.

He'd also used her to show him the exact things he had been saying to Tiffany this evening.

That he could be more, give more, do more than he ever thought, if he had someone behind him believing in him.

"I wish I felt the same," she finally murmured as she stepped away from him. "But...it's just so hard for me to believe. Not to mention, it's so hard for me to imagine myself being a pastor's wife. There are so many other women — Miss Kendall for one — who are so much more qualified than I am. Why wouldn't God choose one of them?"

"You'll have to take that up with him. He doesn't necessarily call people who are qualified. But he qualifies the people He calls. If you let Him."

He tried to fight back his frustration. This would have to be a decision that she would have to make on her own. He couldn't force it on her.

Lord, open her eyes and help her see. Please.

Chapter 19

FRIDAY EVENING TIFFANY paced back-and-forth in front of her front door.

She had been tempted to go all out in getting ready for tonight's date.

She could do it. She knew how to apply makeup perfectly. She had kept a few tailored clothes that she'd pulled out of the bags that she had been going to get rid of.

But that wasn't who she was anymore.

And, over the weeks she'd been in Blueberry Beach, she felt less and less like she needed to use her clothes as armor and more and more like the person she was wasn't such a terrible person who had to hide behind expensive clothes and perfectly applied makeup.

That she could be who she was and not be ashamed.

That God loved her, no matter what.

That... Kane...saw past the baggy clothes and the call girl past and the three husbands and truly did see someone worth loving.

If God could love her, maybe Kane could too.

She stopped, folding her arms over her chest, staring at the wall.

She'd determined to make changes, and she had. Moving to a new place, giving up her old life, which had been easier in a lot of respects than she had expected, and starting down the path that she knew would make her happy, versus the emptiness and soul-sucking shallowness she'd been living in.

But she'd decided, not that long ago, she was going to walk forward with everything she had, going after the family she'd always wanted.

And yet...God had put a man in front of her who wanted her, who thought she was more than what she ever could be, who would love her and support her and encourage her...and with whom she could have the family she wanted, and she was going to turn him down.

And why?

Because he deserved more.

She was being selfless. She was giving up what she wanted, so that he could find someone who was better suited to him.

Everyone has their issues. Maybe Miss Kendall isn't everything you think she is.

She wasn't sure where that thought came from, but she realized immediately it could be true.

Who was she to look at someone and make judgments?

And, who was she to question what the Lord had obviously done. If Kane had wanted Miss Kendall, he had plenty of opportunity. The town tried to get them together. They'd spent months trying to match the two of them up, and they both resisted. Surely that should tell her something. Especially when she came along, and Kane was interested in her.

In fact, Kane was claiming God had put her in his path.

Lord, it's hard for me to imagine that you really have a man like Kane for me. After all the mistakes I've made, and the mess I've made of my life so far. But, if it's really him, show me. Please.

If there's one thing she knew, it was that she didn't want to go into her fourth marriage, without knowing for one hundred percent certain that the person she was with was God's will for her. Because, if...when she said vows again, it would be for the last time.

The sound of a motor broke into her thoughts, and she grabbed her jacket. Shoving her arms in, she squared her shoulders, closed her eyes, took a deep breath, then open the door. Rather than looking for reasons for them not to be together, she was going to spend this evening looking to see if Kane might be right for her.

Kane was out of the car and had just started up the walk when she burst out of the door.

"Excited?" he said with a grin.

"Determined," she said with a lift of her chin.

His brows furrowed, and he tilted his head. "Determined about what?"

"To do God's will."

"And that's why you'll make an excellent pastor's wife. Because of that determination to do right."

She hoped.

"That, and you're a sucker for volunteering for everything. Which is another admirable trait."

He was teasing her now, and she laughed.

He went to her side of the car, opening the door. She murmured 'thank you' and got in, remembering that he had done it before, even when they weren't on a date. That was just the kind of man he was. She had to admit she liked it.

He got in the other side and settled down, starting the car. Although instead of starting off toward town, they started off in the opposite direction and she turned quizzical eyes on him.

"Where are we going?" she asked, curious for sure.

Normally Kane didn't look insecure or even ill at ease, but when he turned his eyes to her, he seemed to be a little vulnerable.

"You said Monday evening when we were babysitting, that you wanted to go somewhere that would just be you and me. Normally, that might mean a picnic on the dunes up the beach, somewhere far where no one else would walk, but since it's so cold out..." His fingers tightened on the steering wheel as he made the turn to the church parking lot.

"I could have taken you to a restaurant, or I suppose we could of gone to a movie or a concert or something normal people do on dates, but...I knew if we went to the church, we'd have the place to ourselves, and...we have a beautiful view of the lake as well."

"We're going on a date to the church?" she said, unable to keep the disbelief out of her tone.

That was definitely a first. And she had been on a lot of dates.

You asked for a sign.

Oh yeah, she had.

"If you don't want to, we can do something else, but I packed all the picnic stuff and...you'll see."

He parked off to the side and hurried around to open her door.

It was charming and sweet and she allowed it, smiling and putting her hand in his as he helped her out.

Maybe they were too old for such things, or maybe they were old enough to appreciate them. She knew she did.

"Can I carry anything in?" she asked.

"Actually I have it all set up," he said, taking her hand, sliding their fingers and lacing them together.

It was a new feeling, not just having Kane's hand wrapped around hers, but feeling the calluses, the roughness, the way it was different than hers, not just bigger, but stronger, more capable. A hand that would protect her and take care of her and provide for her.

But in return, there were things she would need to do.

Things she hadn't even considered in her previous life.

Sure enough, when they walked into the sanctuary, there was a blanket spread out on the floor, right in front of the big picture window in the back, far enough back that they could sit on the floor and look out, seeing the lake stretching endlessly off until it met the horizon.

They would be sitting directly behind where she had used her easel in the parking lot, and spent so many evenings this fall, working on the sunset, never getting it right, but maybe, getting just a little better each time.

Leiklyn and Willan had been extremely encouraging, and had several of her paintings, not just her sunsets, hanging up in the entry of Indigo Inn.

She had sold one for a crazy amount, but she figured it was a fluke.

"Wow." She stopped and took in the blanket with cushions and the picnic basket, the plates and a jug of water sitting on the blanket.

"I figured cushions couldn't hurt. The floor is probably a little harder than the sand on the beach," Kane said, sounding nervous, like maybe he needed to fill the silence with words and she wasn't saying anything and he was eager to know what she was thinking.

"I've never been on a date like this before. I've...honestly never been on a date where the man has put so much thought into it," she said, truly impressed.

And speaking honestly.

"Did someone help you with this?" She turned around and looked at him over her shoulder, asking, not because it was necessarily bad, but...because it did make a difference. If he did it on his own versus doing it because someone had prompted him, or helped him.

"Should I have gotten someone to help me?" he asked.

"No. Not at all. It's amazing and...doesn't seem like something a man would think of."

"Well, to answer your question, I did. I thought of it myself. I did it all myself. And... I'm a little nervous. I was afraid you might not like it. It's not exactly a fancy restaurant."

"I would take this over a fancy restaurant any day. Something you put a lot of thought into, and effort, and did because you cared, something that takes time and energy, rather than just picking up the phone and making reservations. It means a lot." She shook her head, as though if she closed her eyes and open them again it might disappear. "It's just...so unlike anything any man's ever done for me before. I didn't know men could think like this."

"Maybe when a man cares enough about a woman, when that woman occupies so much of his thoughts, so much of his effort, where she's a part of everything he does, he spends a lot of time trying to think of something that would please her and make her smile."

His words were said low, almost as though he couldn't say something that meant so much to him in a normal voice.

His tone made her shiver, in that good way, where it wrapped around her backbone and made her want to move closer to him.

So she did.

It was a date after all, wasn't it?

She turned, and took the one step back so they were standing face-to-face. "I don't even care what the food tastes like, or even if there is any. Just the fact that you thought of this, and went through the trouble of doing it, tells me that I'm important to you."

"That's what I was saying. You're important to me. I think about you all the time. Every day, even when you're not supposed to be volunteering, I listen for your footsteps. When you're in the church, I know where you are, and when you're outside painting," he nodded his head out the window. "It's all I can do to not stand here and watch you the whole time. I don't know what it is about you that just takes everything I am, and makes it want to be with you."

He hadn't even touched her, and already this was the most romantic date she'd ever been on.

"Maybe I shouldn't have admitted that, that I stood and watched you. But I thought this would be a nice place to eat. Not only is the view beautiful, but... I can't stand there and look at it now without thinking of you."

"I had no idea," she said softly.

"I didn't think you did. You probably didn't know that twilight is my favorite time of the day either. One of the things I did before you came, almost daily, was stand here in the church and watch the dance of light and dark, the sun going down, the colors across the sky, God's beauty and handiwork, awed by it every day." He huffed a little breath. "And then you came-"

"And I stood in front of you and ruined your view."

"No. Not at all. You stood in front of me and made my view better. You became everything I wanted, and maybe it was the magic of the twilight, or maybe it was just the mysterious way the Lord works sometimes, but... I don't have any doubts, and I'm just waiting for you to feel the same."

"You can quit waiting. I've felt the same for a long time. I just didn't feel like I would be right for you. Good enough. But..."

"Yeah?" he prompted.

"But I guess your words are getting through to me, or maybe it's the Lord. Although I did ask Him to give me a sign, just anything, to let me know that you really were the one for me."

"And has he?" Kane asked, looking curious, but also confident, like he was so sure that they were supposed to be together, that he knew the Lord would do whatever necessary to assure her of that too.

"I've never been on a date like this before. I've never had a man go through so much effort just to make me happy. I've never felt...cherished like I do now."

His smile was a little prideful, maybe, but also happy, excited, and confident.

"Let's eat," she said, and then stopped mid-turn. "There is food, right?"

"There is. Can't you smell it?"

She sniffed, realizing that she had been smelling it, just hadn't noticed.

"Soup and bread?" she said, breathing deep as she tried to place the scent.

"I know. Not typical picnic food, but it's that time of year.

"I know you didn't make that," she said.

"You're right. I wanted to. It would've been a nice touch, but burnt bread and scalded soup probably wouldn't have been the date you were looking for. Maybe it would have impressed you if I had been able to pull it off, but the odds are good that I wouldn't, and I figured I would rather eat than sit and think about what a nice effort I put into making something that was inedible, though thoughtful."

"I'm in total agreement on that."

"See? You said we had to have things in common. I think we do. We both like to eat."

"I think that might be pushing things a little," she said, as they walked over to the blanket and sat down facing each other, the basket between them.

As he pulled the soup out and poured it into the bowls and she got the water and poured them each a cup, he said, "I have something I wanted to talk to you about."

"Okay?"

"Let's say the blessing first, and maybe you can get a couple of bites of food in before I throw you for a loop again."

Her eyes widened, wondering what in the world he would have to say that could be anymore crazy than the things they'd already talked about.

Was it that bad?

Chapter 20

SO FAR SO GOOD.

Tiffany had seemed happy and impressed with the picnic. And not disgusted like he thought she might be. Like he was being cheap or something.

He hadn't meant it like that at all, and, knowing that she was used to the finer things in life - she admitted she'd married her other husbands for money - he would never be able to give her all the things money could buy.

Not on a small town pastor's salary.

But he thought, was hoping, figured, he might as well find out whether or not it was going to make a difference.

Still, he hadn't done it for that. He'd done it because...because he wanted to share this spot and his favorite time of day with her. Wanted it so badly and wanted her to love it, too.

He supposed that's what it was when you loved someone; you wanted to love the things they loved, and you hoped with all your heart that they would love what you did.

"You had something you were going to ask me?" she said, then she took a bite of her soup. "This is delicious!"

"Iva May. She's an amazing woman, and she's probably the soul of this town. She does far more than people know." He looked at Tiffany and wondered if that would be her.

Not needing it to be, not at all. She was who she was, and he would be completely happy with that, but he could see her being that kind of person. The kind of person who saw a need and took care of it and didn't need a great big fanfare in order to do so. In fact, didn't need to be recognized at all.

"I guess you would know," Tiffany said, looking intrigued, and interested.

Yeah. That would be her.

"Well, I don't really believe in beating around the bush. And, you already know that I'm interested in you. But I suppose," he put a hand up when she opened her mouth to say something. She closed it, and he continued. "I suppose, I need to be honest and say, I've already started the proceedings to adopt Ryan and Haley and Sammy. I've added Isaac to that as well, and although it will take a few months for everything to go through, I don't have any intentions of stopping it."

Her eyes got big, and her lids opened and closed a few times

That didn't alarm him necessarily.

The whole town would probably be shocked when they found out that he - a single man, and a pastor no less – intended to adopt four children.

Tiffany could be surprised. He just hoped when she got over her surprise, she was happy as well.

She coughed a little, almost as though she choked on her soup, and then she shook her head, laughing.

"You would not believe this, but one of the things I had determined was that I was going to go after a family. Somehow. I've set my mind to so many other things, and that was something that watching the children had made me long for. It's something that... I want to contribute to society. Having children and caring about them and making sure that they're taken care of. I wanted that."

"See? We do have a little more in common than what you thought."

"You keep pointing that out. And it's funny, because at the time when we had that discussion to begin with, you were trying to convince me that it was okay that we weren't the same."

"Whatever. Whatever works."

Her wide smile said she felt the exact same way, and the tight ball of anxiety in his chest eased.

"I asked the Lord for a sign. I thought it was the picnic. But, He seems to have seen fit to answer everything. It's kind of unbelievable. I definitely feel like I don't deserve it for sure."

"That's what life is. God constantly giving us what we don't deserve. Hopefully we remember to be grateful for those things."

"Good point. I don't ever want to lose a sense of gratefulness."

"So...you're okay with me adopting children?"

"Of course. You can do whatever you want to," she said, blowing on the soup on her spoon.

"I was hoping...that you might be interested in being their mother." It wasn't a surprise to her. It couldn't be. He hadn't been shy about talking about her being a pastor's wife. If the pastor was going to adopt children, it stood to reason that she would be a pastor's wife and a mother to his children.

"I told you I wanted a family."

"I want you to be a part of my family. Our family. It's not exactly the way families are usually made, but it feels perfect to me. I was hoping you would feel the same."

She tilted her head, swallowing. Then set her spoon down deliberately before looking back up at him, staring into his eyes. "If that's a marriage proposal, it is the strangest one I've ever gotten, and we've already established the fact that I've gotten a lot." Maybe she was joking just a little, but there were also questions in her eyes. Questions he could answer.

"I'm sorry. I guess we've also established the fact that I've never done this before. I did get the picnic right, and the romance of the planning, but the actual popping of the question I did pretty badly, didn't I?"

"I guess I'm not expecting you to be perfect. Especially since you've been so accepting of my flaws."

"Love covers a multitude of sins. Isn't that right?"

"I think that's where the phrase *love is blind* comes from. Maybe we've just twisted it to mean something different. Something almost snide."

"Sure. We say it in an offhand way like, weren't they dumb. But that's really what that verse is saying, when you look at someone with love, that love covers their flaws and makes them look perfect in your eyes."

"That's exactly right. So yeah. I'm all for adopting the children that we've fallen in love with. And yeah, I'll be their mother," she said, almost as though she'd decided that was all the better proposal she was going to get.

He pulled the last small box from the bottom of the basket and scooted around the blanket. It was the perfect time. The sun had been going down, and the brilliant orange of the sunset filled the sanctuary.

"It's kind of hard for me to get down on one knee in front of you when you're sitting beside me. But I'll try."

Her hand went to her heart. "Oh, my goodness."

"You're rushing me a little, but maybe it's my fault for getting the cart ahead of the horse with the kids and everything."

"I think marriage is supposed to come first," she said, kind of absentmindedly, as he shifted so he was on one knee in front of her, with a small box in his hand, which he opened.

"Will you marry me?"

Her eyes were on his face, surprise and happiness floating across her, and then she shook her head, but she said, "Yes."

It was simple and felt right.

"Aren't you going to look at the ring?"

"It doesn't matter what it looks like. I've worn enough of them. And no matter what size the rock is, if there is one, or how expensive, it's not the ring that matters."

"Don't tell me you're not wise. You know more than a lot of people."

"I hadn't thought about it that way, but...maybe you're right." She looked down at the ring and smiled a little. "It seems like an odd tradition to have a ring sitting in front of someone when a man proposes, like it's the ring that convinces them to marry him, rather than the person."

"I don't think we're going to change American tradition today, but I can put it away if it would make you more comfortable."

She giggled, knowing that he wasn't serious, but putting her hand on his forearm anyway. "No. You don't have to do that." Then she sobered. "I'm honored to wear your ring."

"Are you going to look at it now?" he asked, leaning forward just a little.

Her eyes dropped, and then they widened. "It's gorgeous," she said, wonder in her voice.

"It was my grandmother's. Her dad was a jeweler, and when my grandfather wanted to ask her to marry him, he went to her dad, first of all to get permission, and after he had secured that, they designed this ring together. I don't have too much from my family. I was an only child. My parents split when I was little and they seemed to fight as to who had to take me, but my grandmother was a rock until she passed away. Just before she did, she told me she wanted me to have this."

"That's so amazing and special." Tiffany said, sounding awed and impressed.

He had been concerned that she might not want another woman's ring, but the family connection seemed to make it special for her.

"I know. I keep saying about all the times I've done this before, but you know, I have, and the rings have always been big and gaudy and all about making a statement about money. I've never had one that actually meant something. No one has ever given me anything with value beyond the monetary, and...I'm honored."

"I have no idea if it'll fit."

"If it doesn't, we can get it sized."

"You want to try?"

She nodded, and he pulled it out of the box, setting the box aside and slipping it on her finger.

"Perfect," she whispered.

He was thinking the same thing. That she was perfect. The soft orange from the sunset brought out the highlights in her hair and the sparkle in her eyes and the beauty of her smile. But more than that, it seemed to be a reflection of the warmth inside of her. The desire to do good and to do right and to be a blessing in the world.

All things he could see easily. Made more special because they didn't seem to be things that she was aware of or proud of in any way.

He rose to his feet and pulled her up too, not letting go, but gently drawing her into his embrace.

"I didn't really plan for it to happen at this time, but this is my favorite time of day, and I guess if I'm going to ask the one woman in the world who is perfect for me to marry me, and I'm going to do it one time, I'm glad it worked out that this was the time. You're beautiful in the twilight."

"You're handsome all the time. But, that's not really why I fell in love with you."

He stilled for a moment and realized he hadn't said the most important thing.

He put a hand out, brushing her hair away from her face, sliding his fingers down her neck.

"I love you. I love your sweet spirit and your sense of humor. Your desire to do right and your willingness to do anything if it will help someone else. I love the way you give yourself, and the way you always want to be more. I love your humbleness and your willingness to take correction and do whatever it takes to be better."

"No one's ever said anything like that to me before. No one's ever seen any of that in me." She smiled and swallowed almost as though she were trying not to cry.

The light was such he couldn't tell for sure, but her voice was a little wobbly when she said, "I love you too. And I love that you make me want to be better. More. Make me see that I can. Even while I know that if I don't live up to everything you see, you're not going to be disappointed in me, but you're going to keep loving me anyway."

She sighed and slipped her arms around his waist. "I want to be that for you. I want to support you and help you and make you a better version of yourself as well." She shook her head. "Is it cheesy to say you inspire me?"

"I think it's okay for people who love each other to be cheesy with each other," he said softly. Then, he grinned a little as he lowered his head. "I don't care if the entire congregation walks in the door, I'm not jerking back, and I'm not letting go until I've kissed the woman I love."

"I wish I didn't care about that either, but I suppose I would prefer not to have an audience."

"Nothing more than the twilight. And soon that will be gone as well." He lowered his head, and kissed her, pressing her to him, and losing himself in the sweet embrace of the woman he was going to spend his life with.

Epilogue

BILL CLOSED THE SURF shop door, locking it behind him and pulling his coat tighter around him as he walked up the Blueberry Beach sidewalk.

Years ago he'd had a pretty thick head of hair, and a beanie wasn't always strictly necessary in the winter, especially if he let his hair grow a little. But not anymore, as thin as things were getting on the top of his head, a beanie was necessary. He pulled it down over his ears before tucking his hands in his pockets.

His favorite service of the year, the Christmas Eve service, would be starting in just a bit, and he didn't want to be late.

He was an usher and would be handing out candles.

Plus...

Bev would be there. She was every year. It was the one time where she definitely couldn't avoid him.

Even when they met at the diner, or possibly on the street, she could be cool, nodding with reserve before walking away, or busying herself with something else.

Apparently when a person had money, they could dismiss old boyfriends, even if they were boyfriends that they'd had a child with.

He reached the church, half eager, half dreading the inevitable meeting.

Maybe it was Christmas. That magical time of year where miracles seemed possible. Or maybe it was just him getting old and a little feeble in the head, but it felt like there might be a change in the air.

Bev had gone on to be successful without him. He was happy for her.

She'd also been clear on where they stood with each other.

As for him, he'd left her know all those decades ago that if she ever needed him, he was there for her. Wanting her. All she had to do was take him up on it.

She had seemed, if not happy their baby had died, relieved maybe. She had never indicated in any way that she was interested in continuing their relationship.

Of course, what they'd done was wrong, and with him being old enough to know better, he'd let her alone.

Obviously she'd regretted the short relationship they'd had, instigated by her, after he turned her down for months.

He'd grown up in the Upper Peninsula, and hadn't realized how young she was.

She'd lied to him.

Funny that he could still love her, all these years later, knowing she hadn't been honest.

Honesty was a trait he valued, higher than almost any other, except maybe loyalty.

She hadn't been either. Not to him.

The church, glowing candles in the windows, the bits of green at the window sills giving it a cozy look, as warm strings of twinkle lights hung from the ceiling, precluding the need for any other light and adding to the magic of the evening.

Bill had been greeting people for ten minutes, and the church was almost full when Iva May stepped into the back, her arm around a slender woman. Bill's heart started going double time.

Bev.

He handed candles to Adam Coates and his wife Lindy, and their daughter Sierra who was home from college break, smiling and greeting them as they walked by, before he steeled himself.

Normally, he felt like he could act pretty normal around Bev, but that meant he had to hide everything he was feeling inside.

There was no point in letting her know, since she'd been clear about how she felt.

Now that she was successful, she definitely wouldn't be interested in the man who ran a surf shop in a beachside town and for all intents and purposes hadn't really made anything of himself.

"Good evening, ladies," he said, his voice level and calm and totally devoid of the warmth and feeling he wanted to put in it.

"Good evening, Bill," Iva May said, smiling her sweet grandmother smile, her eyes twinkling, her cheeks red from the cold.

"Good evening," Bev said, with just enough frost in her tone to let him know that there wasn't any interest on her part in any further conversation.

"I don't know what you're doing this evening, but if you don't have plans, I was hoping that you and Bev would meet me at my house after the service is over," Iva May said, looking around and lowering her voice just a little. "I've something that I should have said to you years and years ago, and it's been eating me ever since. If you don't mind?" she asked lifting her brows.

Bill looked at Bev, who looked flabbergasted. Whatever she and Iva May had been talking about on their way in, it hadn't been about meeting at Iva May's house with Bill after the service.

"I'm free," he said honestly. Regardless of how Bev felt, he wouldn't say no to Iva May. If she had something she wanted to get off her chest, if she had something she needed help with, if she needed anything, whatever it was, Bill would be there to help her.

He felt like that was his job in Blueberry Beach. Iva May might be the soul of the town, but he was like Santa's elf, going around making sure everything was running smoothly, looking to see where someone needed help, and providing it if at all possible.

When his parents had died, they'd left the property in the Upper Peninsula to him.

It just so happened that it was directly beside property that had become a resort, and he sold it for a good bit. Someone who wanted to build multimillion dollar mansions and rent them out to the vacationing public.

Maybe if he had a wife and children, he would have gone back to the UP and settled there. He loved it, wild and beautiful, but Blueberry Beach was home, and he taken the money and sold the land.

The money had come in handy over the years as he secretly helped people in Blueberry Beach in different ways.

Bev got a lot of the credit for some of the things he'd done, and he was fine with that.

"I suppose I can come. Is it really something you need to tell us both at the same time?" Bev said, her voice sounding cultured and cool and not irritated, necessarily, although he was the only one that knew that she avoided him.

He also didn't think there were too many people in town who knew who the father of her baby had been.

She hadn't told anyone, because he could have gotten in a lot of trouble.

Sometimes the fact that she hadn't made him think that maybe she did care about him.

But there had never been any warmth, any care, any concern in her gaze or in any interaction between them, and he'd lost that hope.

"I do. I need you both," Iva Mae said, and then her smile slipped a little. "Kim should be getting in, and I wanted her to be there as well."

Kim was her daughter, who hardly ever came back to Blueberry Beach, which irritated Bill. And broke his heart a little, because it made Iva May sad. Children should visit their parents and take care of them as they grew older.

Kim was often away, and although she had a family and troubles of her own, it seemed to Bill that a person was neglecting their duties when they didn't take care of their family.

"I suppose I can do it as well," Bev said, managing to sound put out without sounding put out.

Bill supposed he should be offended, but he'd loved Bev for so long that it didn't really matter to him what she said, he just wanted her to be happy. And if that meant she was happy away from him, then that's where she needed to be.

"Is there some problem?" he asked Iva May, ignoring Bev as she ignored him.

"I suppose you could call it that," Iva May said, sounding almost sad, as the piano started playing, and people slowly made their way from where they had been chatting, to their seats in the pews.

More people were lining up behind Iva May and Bev, and Iva May said, "We'd better go. We're in the way. See you after the service at my house. I have hot chocolate, and I have some snacks as well. Come hungry."

"I'll be there," Bill said, knowing that he'd do it for Iva May, but since Bev was going to be there, he wouldn't miss it for the world.

THANKS SO MUCH FOR reading! If you'd like to read the next book in the Blueberry Beach Series, *Tender Mercies*, you can get it HERE[1].

Listen to the professionally produced audio version of this book – for FREE – HERE[2] on the SayWithJay Voiceworks Channel on YouTube.

---

1. https://www.amazon.com/gp/product/B09D2B8GWS

2. https://www.youtube.com/watch?v=hn4NbpEpPBM&list=PLMynUTDTXHZraou-UDUwnhBpnXvE5ap3Uh&index=7

Support our efforts to bring you quality audio at a price that fits into everyone's budget – FREE – check out all the FREE Dyess/Gussman audios HERE[3] **and hit the "Subscribe"** button while you're there. Thanks so much!

Sign up for Jessie's newsletter HERE[4] and find out why readers say, "I eagerly look forward to Tuesday mornings" and "Jessie's newsletter is the only author newsletter that I read every word."

---

3.   https://www.youtube.com/c/SaywithJay

4.   https://dl.bookfunnel.com/97elto4gwl

Tender Mercies

CAN SOMEONE OVER FIFTY still find their soulmate?

Bev became a successful business woman, designing her own line of spandex undergarments for plus sized women and amassing a fortune as the company grew to a multibillion dollar international conglomerate.

If she hadn't lost her baby and broken up with her boyfriend when she was fifteen, none of her financial success would have ever happened.

She really doesn't regret leaving Blueberry Beach and becoming successful. As long as she avoids Bill, the older man whom she'd loved as a teen and the father of her baby.

Bill had never been ambitious and was content to stay in Blueberry Beach and run the surf shop, looking for ways to help his fellow business owners and dispensing wisdom learned from over five decades of living.

He'd been shocked when he found out Bev's age years ago, but he still believed she was his soulmate. Unfortunately, when their baby died, her love for him died, too, and she'd dumped him hard.

He'd married, had children, divorced and wondered if there really was such a thing as a soul mate.

Then, a long held secret from one of the town's pillars is disclosed and directly affects Bill and Bev, destroying everything they thought they believed.

Could they possibly find their soulmates – and a family – in the ashes of their lives?

Order HERE[1] today!

Made in the USA
Middletown, DE
19 August 2023